THE LUNACY
COMMISSION

ALSO BY LAVIE TIDHAR

NOVELS
*The Tel Aviv Dossier**
*Osama**
The Violent Century
*A Man Lies Dreaming**
Unholy Land
By Force Alone
The Candy Mafia

THE BOOKMAN HISTORIES
The Bookman
Camera Obscura
The Great Game
(also available in omnibus form as *The Bookman Histories*)

NOVELLAS
*New Atlantis**
*The Vanishing Kind**
*Cloud Permutations**
*Jesus & the Eightfold Path**
*Gorel & the Pot-Bellied God**

COLLECTIONS
*Black Gods Kiss**
HebrewPunk
The Apex Book of World SF (as editor)
The Apex Book of World SF 2 (as editor)
The Apex Book of World SF 3 (as editor)

*available as a JABberwocky ebook

THE LUNACY
COMMISSION

Lavie Tidhar

JABberwocky Literary Agency, Inc.

The Lunacy Commission

Introduction © 2021 by Silvia Moreno-Garcia

"Red Christmas" © 2016. First published in *Apex Magazine*.
"The Lunacy Commission" © 2020. Original to this collection.
"Killing Kiss" © 2020. First published in *The Book of Extraordinary Impossible Crimes and Puzzling Deaths*.
"A Wonderful Time" © 2019. First published in *The Book of Extraordinary Amateur Sleuth and Private Eye Stories*.
"The Spear of Destiny"© 2017. First published as "My Struggle" in *Apex Magazine*.

Published in 2021 by JABberwocky Literary Agency, Inc, in association with Zeno Agency LTD.

Cover art © 2021 Sarah Anne Langton

ISBN 978-1-625675-23-1

INTRODUCTION

SILVIA MORENO-GARCIA

WHEN THINKING OF writers that have influenced Lavie Tidhar's output, one of the first ones that comes to mind is that colossus of science fiction, Philip K. Dick. Dick's alternate reality World War II novel, *The Man in the High Castle*, bears a semblance to Tidhar's first novel, *Osama*, as well as later works such as *A Man Lies Dreaming* and the parallel reality hopping of *Unholy Land*.

Less mentioned, and perhaps less obvious, are Tidhar's allusions to noir writers, something that becomes clear when flipping through the pages of this collection. Tidhar deploys the hardboiled tactics of writers such as Raymond Chandler, James M. Cain and Dashiell Hammett. That he does it in the form of short stories is even more striking, considering that the noir short story market is not exactly booming. Tidhar obviously likes to go against the grain in more than one way.

If Tidhar were just copying a product, we could call

him an amazing mimic. But he ventures further. Chandler once wrote a line in chapter five of *The Big Sleep* that said "she had the fine-drawn face of an intelligent Jewess." Tidhar's work essentially reworks that line, opens it up, dissecting concerns about Jewishness, about identity, about history, about discrimination, about politics. He does it all while also balancing a bevy of pulp elements.

It's a tough tightrope act, but Tidhar never falls into parody.

If Tidhar had been born a few decades earlier, he'd probably have made a decent living as a noir writer. Maybe he would have even made the jump to Hollywood, since his razor-sharp dialogue seems to be tailor-made for black and white flicks. In our reality, though, he's become the kind of creator you rarely see these days. While most writers are forced to think in terms of the elevator pitch (*Game of Thrones* meets *My Little Pony!*), Tidhar cannot be telegrammed. His work is intelligent, moody, and self-aware.

Adolf Hitler, private detective! Say that out loud and it conjures the sort of premise that seems suitable for a cheap Asylum film rather than a proper science fiction writer. But Tidhar is extremely aware of the power and place of that sort of exploitative entertainment. He loves to blend disparate elements, to thread where others would not, to experiment. His work is a loving nod to the pulp fiction of another era and a scathing critique. It shows a magpie's love of historical tidbits and facts, while never neglecting the beating heart of the story.

Tidhar constructs a gateway into a maze of mirrors that offers, like any good science fiction, a look not of the past despite being set in it, but of our present.

Having known Lavie for more than a decade now, I've long thought I have been lucky to make his acquaintance, and to share lively discussions on literature through the magic of the Internet. As I said in the beginning of this brief introduction, Philip K. Dick was a colossus of science fiction. It's not every day you get to meet someone who will surely be called by a similar name in decades to come. Lavie Tidhar is one of the great writers of my generation and this collection shows a fraction of his might.

—*Silvia Moreno-Garcia, July 2020*

ONE

RED CHRISTMAS

I n another time and place, Shomer still has Fanya and the children. He watches his wife as she lights the Hannukah candles on the windowsill. A hush has settled over the ghetto, and the children, Avrom and Bina, watch the weak, flickering lights of the candle stubs. Shomer watches them too, how they struggle to survive, to hold this flickering flame. He knows that soon, no matter what he'd do, these lights will burn out and die.

But for now, he has them all, and there is no happier man alive than Shomer, that one time purveyor of lurid tales, back when there were still rags to print such nonsense; and after the lighting and the blessing, he takes the children out for a walk. How thin they are, he marvels, watching them spin their makeshift dreidels with the other children, squatting on their haunches in the corner like born gamblers. 'And are we not all gamblers?' he says to Yenkl, who materialises out of the Yiddish Theatre's door, still dressed as *Kuni Leml*. 'Betting against the odds?'

And Yenkl merely nods his head, and rolls a cigarette with long thin fingers. 'They say the trains will soon take all of us all to the east,' he says. 'A promised land of miracles and plenty, eh, Shomer?'

And Shomer knows the children listen, and he knows that he cannot tell them. Rumours only, whispered, of what's happening in the east, what they do to the Jews in those camps in Poland. Rumours only, and surely there can be nothing in them, there can be no truth—

And so his mind shies from the glare of time present and travels elsewhere, to another time and place of his own making, and to a sordid little tale of shund, that is to say, of pulp—of blackmail, violence, and murder.

1

SHE PUFFED ON the cigarette with quick, nervous jerks of her hand. The fur coat she wore was mottled in places and her big, dark eyes looked at me with a sort of nervous excitement. 'I am being blackmailed, you see, Herr Hitler.'

I hated the smell of tobacco. I hated the cold of my office, above the Jew baker's shop. I hated London, and this cold, soulless island on which I'd found myself, a refugee. I hated what I had become.

'It's Wolf, now,' I told her. 'The name. Just Wolf.'

She shrugged. She didn't care who or what I was.

You probably wouldn't remember her, now. I will call her Elske Sturm, though that was not her real name, exactly. She often played the kind of girl who drowned at the end of the movie. Sometimes I wished a rain would come and drown the whole world, and everything in it. Once, I was going to conquer the world. Now I was a piece of gum stuck to a *spassmacher*'s shoe.

I said, 'Blackmail, *Fraulein* Sturm?'

'I have been sent pictures,' she said. 'Compromising photographs. The blackmailer threatens to, well, you can connect the dots.'

'Is there any more?' I said. There usually was.

She shrugged. It was a very Teutonic shrug. 'The... other person in the photographs,' she said. 'He's married.'

'I see.'

'We're in love.' She said it like it meant nothing, and she was right, because it never does. It was just an ugly case of adultery, the kind I wouldn't usually touch, but I needed the money. It was December, 1937, and it was a cold winter and only going to get worse. I was behind on my rent and down on my luck, and the old wound from the concentration camp the communists had put me in after my Fall ached in cold weather.

'Who is the other party?'

'I'd rather not mention his name,' she said quickly. 'He is a prominent politician.'

'...I see.' And I did. She was just an actress, and no one expects high morals from a simple bird of paradise. They were pretty and empty headed, and dirty pictures would just as likely help their careers as ruin them. '... Does he know?'

She shrugged. 'I don't know,' she said in a flat voice. 'We haven't spoken about it.'

She was lying, of course. She was never that good an actress. I took down the details. She had met with this man three times in different hotels around London. The blackmailer must have followed them, snapped photographs through the window of one of the rooms. I could imagine it easy enough. I said, 'Do you have the note?'

'Yes. Here.' She pushed it across my desk. The message was short: *Bring £300 in notes, Leave the bag by the Eleanor Cross, Sunday, 1pm, come alone, I will be watching you. No funny stuff.*

'I had to look up the Eleanor Cross,' she said. 'It's that hideous monument outside Charing Cross Station.'

I nodded. I knew the place. I myself had arrived in London into that cesspit of racial impurity that was Charing Cross. It had become the gateway into London for us refugees from the Fall. The Jews and the communists held Germany now in their filthy hands, and good, honest *Volk*, proud Aryans, were now the scum of Europe, beggars arriving on the filthy shores of England cap in hand. How I hated them! How I hated them all!

'You will make the drop? Alone?'

She bit her nails. 'If that's what you'd advise.'

'It is.'

'And you will…?'

'I will be there. You won't see me.'

'I would be ever so grateful,' she said. She shimmered over to me. She draped herself over my desk and crossed her long pale legs, one over the other. 'I remember you from the old days,' she said. 'I saw you speak once, in Munich. You were so magnetic on stage. When you spoke, I really believed in you, we all did, I think. You said Germany could be great again.' She sighed. 'But I guess you were wrong after all.'

'Germany was betrayed!' I said. 'I would have led her to victory, to, to…!' Words failed me. She smiled at me pityingly. Her long fingers reached down and curled around my collar. Her nails were painted crimson. She was a cheap whore like all actresses are. Her perfume mixed with the smell of her cigarette as she leaned close into me. Her lips were red and ripe for the picking. 'I would be so grateful for your efforts…' she said.

With an effort I pushed her away. I liked my women the way I liked my dogs, vicious and submissive at once. 'I shall see you Sunday,' I said, coldly. 'A retainer of five pounds would suffice, Fraulein Sturm.'

For a moment her eyes flashed; then she laughed, her tongue darting in between those white teeth of hers, as though she held me in contempt. She took the money out of her purse and laid it on my desk.

'Is that all,' she said.

I let it go past me. These days, I let a lot of things slide.

'*Auf Wiedersehen,*' I said.

She nodded, wordlessly. Then she left my office, slamming the door shut in her wake. I guess for a woman of her kind seduction was just another transaction on the balance sheet of life, like buying bread or paying off a blackmailer. I sat there for a long moment, thinking of all I had lost. Then I got up, retrieved my raincoat and my fedora, and followed her.

2

A DRUNK SANTA Claus bumped into me as I crossed Shaftesbury Avenue, his disgusting breath rancid on my face.

'*Scheisse!*' I said, trying to push him off. He staggered but stood his ground, and stared at me with mean little eyes.

'Filthy foreigners,' he mumbled. 'Why don't you all just f—k off back to your own country.'

Before I could reply I saw a couple of bobbies in uniform turn and look our way.

'Forget it,' I said, and began to walk away. He sneered behind me.

'Run away now, little Kraut!' he shouted. I hated his entire race at that point. Hate was a powerful motivator, it had once made me great, and it sustained me, still. I nearly went back at him, but the bobbies were watching, and I had my job, still.

I don't know why I was following Elske. I did not quite believe her story. I followed her to Sakall's, near the Hippodrome, on Little Newport Street. Sakall's was one of the fashionable new establishments, opened by a Hungarian bit part actor, and it catered to many of the performers who trod the Hippodrome's stage. There were usually a couple of photographers stationed outside, and I recognised Hoffmann, who I used to be friendly with back in Munich. He waved when he saw me. There was a bottle of cheap red wine by his feet, which he raised in greeting at my approach. Already, he was quite drunk.

'Wolf,' he said. 'It is good to see you.'

'Hoffmann.'

'We have fallen on hard times, eh, my friend?' He gave me a sardonic salute, arm extended, and chuckled. He was in his fifties and a good Aryan, and he had always served me well. 'Yet still we carry on.'

I ignored him and his little jokes and fixed my eyes on the entrance to Sakall's. The actress, Elske, disappeared inside. Hoffmann watched me watch her and chuckled again. 'She's a nice bit of totty and no mistake,' he said.

'Do you know who she's meeting?'

'Sure, sure. Some big shot out of Hollywood, one of those Warner brothers.'

'A Jew?'

He shrugged. 'Who isn't a Jew, these day,' he said.

'Is she looking for a job?'

'Rumour has it she's desperate to get out. California, Wolf!' he said. 'Picture it, the sand beaches and the palm trees and the girls…'

'California,' I told him coldly, 'is filled with dirty Jews.'

'Sure, sure,' he said. 'But that's show business.'

It was cold. I rubbed my hands together, stamped my feet, but it didn't really help. I remembered the cold of the Great War, the trenches and the stench of men's fear. It is easier to be cold when one is younger.

'Do you know if she's seeing anyone?'

'Seeing?' he said. 'I do not know about *seeing*. But word is she plays footsie with half the eligible bachelors of London. And they're not always bachelors, either, if you get my meaning.'

'Anyone in particular?' I said, without much interest.

He shrugged, then brightened up suddenly. 'That young whippersnapper of yours,' he said. 'That Heydrich.'

'Heydrich?' I said. '*Reinhard* Heydrich? Himmer's man?' I remembered him, vaguely. A thin faced former musician with a high pitched voice, who got kicked out of the Navy for conduct unbecoming of a gentleman. I remembered his wife better than him, Lina, a pleasant enough wench who was charmingly anti-Semitic. She almost came in her drawers every time she met me. She was the one who sent her husband for the job interview with Himmler.

'He was in charge of intelligence, as far as I remember. He would have made a good detective if only he could keep it in his pants from time to time.'

'Who of us can,' Hoffmann said, philosophically.

'But what is he doing in London? I thought the communists had him.'

'He got out even before the Reichstag burned,' Hoffmann said. 'He was always a practical man, as far as I remember.'

I could not even blame him, I realised. I had surrounded myself with ruthless, efficient men. Their loyalty was not in question—they had always been loyal first and foremost to themselves.

'He's got a place in town, as far as I know,' Hoffmann said. 'Wife and kids and all. I don't know what he does, exactly. Something in the movies. A guy like him's bound to land on his feet.'

I nodded, thoughtfully.

'Thanks, Hoffmann,' I said.

'You going to stick around?'

'No,' I told him. 'I think I saw all I needed to see.'

'Go well, Wolf,' he said. 'Go in peace.'

'We both,' I told him, 'know that's unlikely.'

I could hear his chuckles all the way until I turned the corner.

3

I HEADED DOWN Charing Cross Road to the train terminus. I wanted to see the drop point for myself. The night had thickened about me and the London fog rose from the pavements and made the movements of people seem like a sort of shadow play. Hoffman used to have a studio in Munich, but when the communists took Germany he ran. Many of my old comrades did, escaping like rats, and now they infested this town with their presence. Passing St Martin-in-the-Fields I could hear carol singers, and a beggar shook his metal bowl at me, hoping for alms that weren't going to come. I could hear the whistle of the trains as they crossed over the river, my native tongue being spoken, the shrill cries of a boy selling the *Evening Standard*, the drunken laughter of revellers at a nearby pub.

I did not see the two men in the black uniform of the British Fascists. They blended perfectly into the dark.

When I reached sight of the station I stopped and simply stared. The Eleanor Cross was surrounded by recent arrivals, all milling about like cattle. The cross, I remembered, had been erected as an act of love, one of twelve monuments King Edward had put up in memory of his late wife. I hated sentimental fools. When Geli killed herself, with my own gun, I was outraged at her betrayal. How dared she defy me in this way!

I stared at the monument, thinking. It was a nice, busy spot. Easy to disappear in a crowd. I could see why the blackmailer chose it. I decided to buy myself a cup of hot chocolate, since I had money in my pocket for once. I had always had a fondness for sweet things. I turned, which was when I saw them. There were two of them and they were ugly in that English sort of way, as though they raise the boys alongside the pigs. They wore black with the jagged lightning bolt of the British Union of Fascists on the breast, and they had bad teeth, bad breath, and nasty grins.

'Going somewhere?'

'Excuse me, fellows,' I said, trying to look round them for an avenue of escape—just as the one on the right sank his fist into my stomach and knocked all the air out of me.

'No need to apologise, old boy,' the one on the left said pleasantly. He had a cosh in his hand.

'No, don't—'

It came down and connected with the back of my head. Pain exploded behind my eyes, and a million yellow stars swam in my field of vision and were replicated sixfold; but luckily I lost consciousness at that point.

4

'SO YOU'RE THE Charlie Hunt who's been messing with my girl,' the man said.

'Eh?' I said, confused.

'He means you're a c—'

'That's enough, Reggie.'

My head felt like a football that's been kicked round in No Man's Land during the Christmas Truce. I looked around me, carefully. I was in a dark warehouse of some sort. On the walls I could see posters for Oswald Mosley, the Smethwick MP and leader of the BUF. He had a thin aristocratic face and a thin moustache and a ghoul's smile. *Re-Elect Mosley!* Said the posters.

I was bound to a chair. Standing above me were the two Fascist goons and a third man. He wore a good suit, with lightning strike cufflinks, and he looked down on me with bloodshot eyes.

'Who the *f—k* are you?' I said.

He backhanded me. My head snapped sideways and the pain burned like a flame and I thought a tooth might have come loose.

'I'm the one asking the questions here!' he said.

I spat out blood, just missing his shoes, and he backhanded me again.

'What were you doing with my girl?' he said.

'Elske?'

'You're not worthy to speak her name!'

He slapped me again. I was getting tired of it. Like Germany, a man can only take so much before he must resort to violence.

I wanted very much to kill him at that moment.

His two boys stood on either side of him and looked at me with amused butcher boys' grins.

'Fat pigs,' I said, and tried to spit again, but there wasn't much in me.

'Who are you?' the man in the suit said.

'Wolf,' I said. 'My name's Wolf. I'm a private eye.'

'A what?' he said, sounding confused.

'A P.I. A gumshoe. A shamus. A dick!'

He looked even more confused, if that were possible. They don't breed them for intelligence, in England, so much as for a sort of bovine endurance.

'You mean, like in Agatha Christie?' he said.

'No, not like f—king Agatha Christie,' I said, though really I was secretly very fond of her books. 'More like Sam Spade.'

'I don't know what in God's name you're talking about,' he said, but he looked a little less mad, all of a sudden. 'Why were you seeing Elske?'

'She hired me,' I said.

Understanding dawned on his face, and then something else, too, a sort of look I recognised and didn't much like. He shook his fat finger in my face. 'You look kind of familiar,' he said.

'It's just the light,' I said.

'No, no,' he insisted. 'You look like—no, you can't be! I thought you were dead.'

'I get that a lot,' I told him.

He was beaming down on me now. 'I don't believe it!' he said. 'Boys, untie our guest. I'm so sorry, Mr—'

'Wolf,' I said, tiredly. 'It's just Wolf, now.'

'You could have led all of Germany!' he said.

'I was betrayed. Germany–!' Tears choked my voice.
'Germany has been prostituted, and I—'

'Take it easy, old fellow,' he said. His boys untied me.
I rubbed my arms, trying to get my circulation back. I
was getting too old for this scheisse.

'Elske told you? About the letter?'

I said, 'So you're the second party.'

'I'm sorry we got off on the wrong foot,' he said. 'I'm
William Joyce.'

Now I knew why he seemed familiar. It was his voice,
you could often hear it on the radio. He was the BUF's
Director of Propaganda, Mosley's very own cut-rate
Joseph Goebbels. The way things were going, the British
Fascists were going to win the next general election in a
couple of years.

'So you're being blackmailed?' I said. 'Only Elske gave
me the impression it was her that the blackmailer was
targeting.'

'Her!' He laughed, an unsettling sound like a gas
explosion. 'She's an actress, and they never have any
money of their own, Wolf.'

I nodded, though that was a mistake. My head felt
very sore. I said, carefully, 'So *you* are the party being
blackmailed?'

'Of course.' He made a dismissive gesture. 'D—ned
vultures. A man in my position is always in danger of
being pursued. No doubt it would turn out to be a Jew
behind it. Mark my words.'

'And you intend to give Elske the money?'

He shrugged. 'The problem with blackmailers, Wolf,' he said sagely, 'is that they're never satisfied with just one drink. They have to keep milking the cow–' and he made a rude jerking motion with his fist. Then he looked at me, with those cold, English eyes. 'You say Elske hired you? I say good. A man of your keen analytical skills, your ruthless dedication—I couldn't have made a better choice myself.'

He shook my hand, then patted me on the back. 'You can make your own way back, can't you?' he said. He ushered me out of the room and down a corridor and out a back door and waved me goodbye cheerily enough. I found myself standing on Whitehall, outside one of those anonymous government buildings the purpose of which you never know; they could be anything, really. Big Ben was chiming the hour. It was late; I was cold; my head hurt diabolically. And a passing dog, stopping to sniff me, took a s—t on my shoes before running off.

So I went home.

5

SEVERAL THINGS WERE obvious to me. That I was being played, was one. That the players themselves were being played was another. It had sounded like just a little dirty bit of blackmail to begin with, but things are seldom this simple in real life.

'So you see?' I told Martha. 'It all makes perfect sense, in a way, don't you think?'

She glared at me, then farted. I was shaving in the shared bathroom in the hall and she was waiting for me to finish, with arms crossed, growing visibly impatient. She was a corpulent old crone who sold poisoned seeds for passers-by to feed the pigeons in Trafalgar Square. I quite liked the old mass murdering bitch. In a way, she was the only friend I had in this world.

'You think this Heydrich guy is blackmailing this William Joyce guy?' she said.

'Exactly.'

'And you think Joyce sent this Elske woman to hire you, and then had you kidnapped?'

'Exactly!' I said. 'It's the old carrot and stick. He must be really worried about it, under all that bluster. Do this and I reward you, don't do this and…' I rubbed my head, where a sore bruise still very much lingered. 'You get the picture.'

'I don't get s—t,' she said. 'Are you finished in there?'

'I'm shaving,' I said. I touched my upper lip, tenderly. I used to have a moustache, but it was gone, now. I still missed it, sometimes. But it belonged in the past.

'Listen, Wolfy,' she said. 'Old Martha really needs to have a s—t, and soon.' She farted again and then laughed delightedly. 'You shave like a prostitute,' she said.

'Listen to me, you disgusting old bat!' I screamed, waving my safety razor threateningly at her. 'You don't seem to see the bigger picture here!'

'Ah oh,' she said. She clutched her stomach and pushed past me into the bathroom despite my protestations, and before I could do anything to stop her she dropped her drawers and sat down on the toilet and I heard a vile, awful sound as she emptied her bowels. As the smell threatened to choke me, I tactically withdrew into the corridor, still holding the useless razor in my hand. Martha looked up at me and smiled dreamily. 'I'm sure it will all work out, Wolf. It sounds like you have everything very much in hand.'

6

IT WAS ABOUT eleven o'clock in the morning, on a cold and miserable December just shy of Christmas Eve. I couldn't care less about Santa Claus, and the only Rudolf I knew was Hess. I wore my old rain mac and my beat up fedora, and the shoes the dog had taken a s—t on. I had a bump on my head, a Luger in my coat, and a heartfelt desire to be elsewhere. I was everything a private detective ought to be. I was looking after three hundred pounds.

Charing Cross Station was crowded by the time I got there. The trains were pulling in from Dover, and they dislodged their cargo of refugees at the platforms, so that the poor fools, the remains of their former lives bundled into cheap suitcases, stood blinking in the weak English light and wondered what the hell they were doing here. There is nothing worse than the daylight in England, it turns everyone into ghosts.

Policemen moved among the throng, keeping an eye out for pickpockets and breaking fights. Relatives waiting anxiously scanned the oncoming faces for long lost loved ones and, when found, engaged in a human orgy of celebration that I found distasteful. This was the great rabble of Europe, fleeing the communists. I loathed them, I would have exterminated them all if only I could.

The whole place was in chaos. I thought I saw the two Fascists who were in Joyce's employ, but it was impossible to keep track of anything or anyone. Elske pushed through the crowds, carrying the money, dressed anonymously enough that no one thought to associate her with the glamorous figure she presented on screen. Carol singers mingled with a variety of Father Christmases and cab drivers and stuggering drunks from the nearby pubs. I lost sight of Elske just as she was standing by the monument, and only for a moment.

I pushed through the crowds towards her and when it parted I saw that the satchel she had carried was gone.

7

FOR A MOMENT I panicked. Then I caught sight of him, moving away with a sort of smooth certainty that made the crowd flow around him like water. He was dressed in red and white, but he wasn't fat, not at all. He was a blade of a man and for a moment he turned his head and looked back, and our eyes met.

Recognition flared in his eyes, and with it came a sardonic smile. Then he pushed through the throng, away from the station and onto the Strand, and I lost sight of him. I gave chase, shouting at the people to move out of my way, cursing as they shuffled and stood their ground like the livestock that they were. Nevertheless I gained ground and, emerging onto the busy street near Coutts Bank I caught sight of him again, hurrying with long, assured strides past the British Medical Association Building. I ran, passed the Adelphi, and saw him turn unhurriedly to enter the Savoy on the other side of the street.

'Reinhard!' I yelled. 'Reinhard, d—n it!'

I pulled out my gun. I do not know what I would have done, whether I'd had shot him. It made no difference, in the end.

He turned at the sound of my voice. Again that smile briefly illuminated his face, cold and mocking. I couldn't see the satchel. He began to raise his arm, perhaps in greeting, perhaps in a mocking salute of the kind they used to give me.

The car came out of nowhere.

It was a sleek black Daimler with its headlights shining through the fog. It hit Reinhard Heydrich's body with a sickening crunch and didn't stop. His body rolled and the car drove over it and sped away in the direction we'd just come from. I ran across to him. He lay there on the dirty ground, in the sludgy grey-white snow. His blood was very red under the streetlights.

He tried to smile.

'Wolf,' he said. 'It has been... a while.'

'I thought you had more sense than that,' I told him.

'It was just a... bit of blackmail,' he said. 'She put me up to it, you know.'

'Elske? Yes, I figured as much.'

'She was... good in the sack.' He coughed, and blood came gurgling out of his mouth, staining his white teeth. 'I guess she... played me for a fool.'

I didn't know what to tell him. That this wasn't how it was meant to end? Heydrich was a rat, and he'd been killed like a rodent, and it was nothing more than he deserved, perhaps than any of us deserve, if you come down to it. I watched him die. He died well, I'll give him that. I searched his body, quickly.

Then I got out of there before the police came.

8

THERE WAS A small Christmas tree on Berwick Street visible from my office; its lights illuminated the whores who congregated on that side of the street and threw elongated, talon-like shadows over the furtive punters. On the other end of the road there were children, squatting by the corner, gambling over the outcome of a spinning top. I hated them all.

Her perfume preceded her into my office. She stood in the doorway and surveyed the room and then lit up a cigarette.

'It's terrible,' she said. 'What happened.'

'Fraulein Sturm.'

'Poor Heydrich. I never suspected—'

'Of course not,' I said.

'William was *most* grateful for your services,' she said. She reached into her handbag and came out with a handful of notes and passed them to me. I had no choice. I took them.

'He is a very important man, you know,' she said. 'They say Sir Oswald will become prime minister in the next elections, and William is going to be his right-hand man. He thinks the world of you, you know. You were always such an inspiration for their cause.'

'The money,' I said, ignoring her prattling. 'It wasn't on him.'

'I beg your pardon?'

'The pay-off. It was missing.'

She shrugged. 'He must have hidden it somewhere.'

'Perhaps.' I noticed, behind her in the corridor, a packed suitcase. 'Going someplace, Fraulein?'

'Los Angeles,' she said. 'The ship sails tomorrow morning. I am just on my way to the train station.' She smiled at me round her cigarette. 'I've been offered a contract with one of the movie studios.'

'You would work for Jews?' I said.

'A girl's gotta eat.'

'Your earrings,' I said. 'Are they new? They look expensive.'

She laughed, gaily. 'I treated myself,' she said, with no self-consciousness. 'I must look my best, for the photographers.'

'Of course.'

When she left I stared at the money she'd left me. I knew she'd used Heinrich to blackmail Joyce, and that, having got her hands on the money she needed, manipulated Joyce into eliminating Heydrich. I felt a grudging admiration for her. She was cool as Andersen's Snow Queen, as nasty as any National Socialist. A woman like that, I thought, could go far in show business.

Then I slid out the envelope that's been sitting in my drawer. The ever helpful Hoffmann had developed the negatives for me, the ones I had taken off of Heydrich's corpse. I looked at the photos dispassionately. The naked couple portrayed in them was captured in stark relief, entwined in a variety of poses. As a study in animal reproduction they would have made for excellent woodcuts.

I tapped my fingers on the desk. A thought slowly stole into my head. It was a cold December, and it was only going to get colder. And as Elske had so eloquently put it, a girl's gotta eat.

I took a sheet of blank paper, picked up a pen and, slowly, I began to write.

You killed the wrong man. I have the negatives. Bring £500. Come alone. I will be watching you…

I stared at the note for a while, then added, in a post-script, *No funny stuff.*

When I raised my head it had begun to snow outside the window; the snow fell in delicate shivers on the hard cold ground, and in the distance the bells began to toll. I rubbed my hands together to keep them warm. Old Martha stuck her head through the door and hiccupped. She was quite intoxicated. 'Fancy a drink, Wolfy?' she said.

'I don't drink,' I told her.

'Oh, come on,' she said, 'it's the holidays.'

She disappeared and I could hear her heavy steps going back to her room. I was so cold, and it was going to be a cold winter. After a moment I got up, folded the note neatly and placed it in an envelope. I would mail it tomorrow, I thought. I put it in my coat pocket and left the office and went and knocked on Martha's door.

'Come in,' she purred.

I sighed and went inside. She was sprawled in her armchair, covered in a dirty blanket, with half a bottle of gin in her hand.

She raised it in salute as I sat down.

'Merry Christmas, Wolf,' she said.

* * *

IN ANOTHER TIME and place, Shomer watches the children. It begins to snow, then, a beautiful, clean phenomenon, and the children run and laugh in the ghetto streets, and later play making snow angels. He worries how to keep them warm, he worries if they'll have food enough to eat, this winter, and he's inexplicably fearful of trains, the trains that depart full from the Umschlagplatz, *but always return empty.*

He would do anything to keep them safe, to keep them warm, he would do anything to hear their laughter: but he also knows that while one may find an escape in What-Ifs, in flights of fancy, such an escape is only possible in one's imagination. Ultimately, he thinks, though it breaks his heart, all such fantasy is futile.

But for now, they are here, they are together, on this night of Hannukah. When they return home, the candles have burned out, and everywhere is dark. He puts the children to bed, and covers them, and sits with them as they fall asleep. His wife comes and sits with him, and he holds her hand.

'Oh, Fanya,' he says. 'Fanya, they're so beautiful!'

TWO
THE LUNACY COMMISSION

I n another time and place Shomer listens to the radio.
They have that—they have that still—and as the
notes of the Warsaw National Philharmonic Orchestra's performance of Berlioz's "Simphonie Fantastique" fill
the air, Shomer closes his eyes. In the music he can forget
the ghetto, the war, the worry of the fate of those sent east
for what the Nazis term 'resettlement'. In a corner of the
room his daughter, Bina, turns and sighs in her sleep.
How sweet the sound of her voice. Earlier she had complained of hunger, and he, her father, said nothing, for
what could he have said?

Now he wants only to escape, but there is no escape, not
from this place, not at this time. And so he shuts his eyes and
flees into another place and time. It's fantasy, where things
are always simpler.

1

JOYCE'S BREATH ALREADY stank with booze and it was barely noon. I stared at the deep ugly scar that ran from his earlobe to the corner of his mouth. He told people the scar was from a Jewish knifeman who objected to his anti-Semitic views, but the truth was one of his mistresses gave it to him. That, and one could only hope, the clap.

He stared at me thoughtfully. His name was William Joyce but everyone called him Lord Haw-Haw.

'You really could have been somebody, if it weren't for those bloody Jews.'

I did not want to discuss ancient history with that awful man. Needless to say I had once been someone, at least until the communists stole the 1933 elections in Germany and threw me in a concentration camp. I had managed to escape, and made my way to England, that god-forsaken island across the channel from Europe, and there I eked out a miserable living as a private eye. The year was 1938 and it was winter, it always was in London, that great cesspool into which all the loungers and idlers of the Empire are irresistibly drained. Those weren't my words, but those of that detective writer, Conan Doyle. The man believed in fairies and spirits and went to his death-bed still believing in communication with the after-life, the idiot.

Me, I liked my dead silent and in the dirt where they belonged.

'What, exactly, do you want, *Herr* Joyce?' I said.

'Come, come,' he said. 'I have to admit, I was curious.'

'Curiosity,' I said, 'killed the cat.'

He laughed. 'Don't worry about me,' he said. 'I have nine lives.'

It was the sort of cheap dialogue you'd get on *The Adventures of Ellery Queen* on Radio Luxembourg.

'Then have you satisfied your curiosity?' I said. 'We *have* met before.'

I had done a job a couple of months back for the man's former mistress.

'Only briefly,' he said. 'I didn't get a good look at you then and, I have to admit, you are not quite what I expected.'

'I am not the man I was.'

'You look different, without the moustache.'

I shrugged, wishing he'd get on with whatever was on his mind.

'Do you never miss it, Wolf?' he said.

I thought of Nuremberg, the crowds amassed in the square as I stood on the podium, delivering a speech, rallying them up... how *glorious* it all was! I, who could have been ruler of all of Germany—no, of the world!

'I don't think about the past.'

'A shame. Well, to business, then,' he said. 'I am looking for a woman.'

'You can hire one down by the Adelphi, by the hour,' I said. 'Just make sure to wear a Frenchie on your *schwanz*.'

Instead of taking offence, the loathsome fellow beamed at me delightedly.

'Why, you really *are* a man of the world!' he said. 'But be that as it may, Wolf, I hardly need to pay for it, old bean.'

'That's what they all say.'

'Come, come. You are a detective. Deduce, man!'

I stared at him, thinking. The only thing I could really make out was that he was drunk—but then, weren't they all?

'Let's see,' I said. 'You are a radio broadcaster with a large following—the Lord Haw-Haw Halftime Hour is a popular show here in Britain—'

'Sponsored by Bayer,' he said, automatically. 'Drugs You Can Trust. And trust me—' he tapped his nose, 'they're good. You want some? They do this methamphetamine mix that makes Pervitin look like Cola candy.'

'Maybe later. Thanks. Shall I proceed?'

'Please.'

'Because the BBC won't allocate commercial licenses to other radio stations to operate in the UK, you are by necessity based on the continent. Is that correct?'

'Correct.'

'Then can I surmise that the *Fraulein* in question is most likely not British?'

He was smiling. 'You can.'

'And knowing your views on racial purity, she is an Aryan—'

'Of course—'

'Most likely German. Or else why ask for me?'

He clapped, slowly. 'Remarkable,' he said, with a true note of admiration.

'She is most likely young—'

His smile grew wider at that.

'And poor, or was. A refugee from the Soviet regime in Germany.'

'Not unlike yourself,' he said, but I ignored him.

'You no doubt dazzled her with your fame and your money—'

'The drugs don't hurt, either,' he said.

'Then, what? Sent her off to England? But that won't work, or you wouldn't be looking for her. Unless she got away… that's right, isn't it? She used you and then vanished—which meant she had something to fall back on, in England. Not a man, I'd wager… some sort of trade?'

The smile left his face.

I took a stab at it, and scored.

'If I had to guess, I'd say a nurse.'

'Impressive, Mr Wolf!'

I shrugged. 'So what,' I said, 'does she owe you money? Or is it that you want her back?'

'That whore,' he said. 'After all I've done for her. No, don't worry, Wolf, it's nothing like that. The b—ch stole something of mine and I need it back. It's a small thing, of little consequence. But I want it back all the same.'

'Then you know where she is?'

'I do.'

'But you can't get to it.'

'I can't.'

I stared at him, wondering what the catch was, knowing there was one. There always was, with a piece of human garbage like Lord Haw-Haw.

He smiled at me again, with all those white teeth.

'How would you like a pleasant little holiday in the country?' he said

2

'SCHEISSE!' I SCREAMED. 'Scheisse! Let go of me!'

The two orderlies in the white coats ignored me. They had me wrapped up in a straightjacket. I was no Axel Hellstrom, I couldn't open locks with the power of my mind. I struggled against my bond, but in vain.

'*F—king* Lord Haw-Haw,' I said, with feeling.

'I *love* his show on Radio Luxembourg,' the orderly on the left said.

'*So* funny,' said the orderly on the right. 'Did you hear the one about the German refugees trying to cross the channel he told the other day?'

'What do you call ten thousand refugees at the bottom of the sea?'

'A good start!'

They both laughed like diseased dogs, and I wondered how it had come to this. Then they led me into the building and the heavy doors shut behind us with a very final sort of note, and I was officially incarcerated in the insane asylum.

The Brookwood Hospital occupies a large chunk of pristine countryside outside Woking, in Surrey. It is a large, draughty building, designed by Charles Henry Howell, who was the principal architect for the Lunacy Commission. I had been admitted as an inmate. This was all part of Lord Haw-Haw's plan.

'If we take it off do you promise not to make trouble?'

'I'll be good,' I said.

They removed the straightjacket and I massaged my wrists. A nurse in a bright white coat came over to examine me.

'What's his thing?' she said.

'He thinks he's Adolf Hitler.'

She looked at the orderly blankly. 'Who?'

The orderly shrugged.

She took my blood pressure and listened to my heart and wrote something in a chart and then led me through the large common room, where various inmates lounged about in robes, listening to the radio. "My Funny Valentine" was playing. The nurse led me to a room with two beds and a sink. A short fat man was sitting on an unmade bed and looked up at me mournfully as I came in. He was smoking a cigar.

'You don't want to be here,' he said. 'They're all crazy round here.'

'Who the hell are you?'

'You'll be sharing the room with Mr Spencer,' the nurse said. 'This is Mr Spencer.'

'It's Churchill, actually,' the fat man said. 'Winston Churchill. Former First Lord of the Admiralty and Chancellor of the Exchequer.' He waved the cigar modestly. 'Also an author.'

I stared at the fat man, then at the nurse. She shrugged. 'I'll leave you two to it,' she said. 'Don't worry, Mr Spencer is harmless enough.'

With that she took her leave. I sat down on the unoccupied bed.

'Churchill, huh?'

'My enemies have conspired against me, to falsely imprison me in this nuthouse,' the fat man said, as though it should be perfectly simple even to a moron. 'Mosley and his gang of Fascist thugs! They'd had me kidnapped and committed here under false pretences, for fear that I would unite the country against their evil!'

'You sound like a crazy person.'

He glared at me and puffed on his cigar. 'Who the hell are you?'

'Wolf,' I said, tiredly. 'Just call me Wolf.'

He shrugged, then leaned in and spoke in a hushed voice. 'Listen,' he said. 'We have to get out of here.

Warn the government of what's going on. They'll listen to me, I'm an important man, I could have been the Prime Minister you know.'

'Sure,' I said. 'Sure.' I wasn't any closer to my goal and the smoke from his cheap cigar was making me nauseous. 'Listen, Spencer—'

'I told you, I'm Winston bloody Churchill!'

'—Whoever you are, what's the deal here? How does it all work?'

He subsided at that. 'It's not so bad, really,' he said. 'They treat us well. Food's not awful and there's the radio, and bridge or chess—do you play?'

'From time to time.'

He brightened at that. 'We should play sometime.'

'Sure,' I said. 'Sure.'

'There's three meals a day and they give us pills if we get uppity. It's best not to get uppity, Wolf. They don't like that. They like everything to be peachy, you know?'

'Uppity? Peachy? What are these words? What are you blathering on about, man!'

'They just want peace and quiet,' he said.

'And the nurses?' I said.

'The nurses? Don't trust them.' Again he leaned forward, like he wanted to impart a secret. 'Don't trust *anyone!*' he straightened up and gave me a tight smile wrapped around his cigar. He nodded at the walls. 'They're *listening*,' he said, so softly I barely heard him.

'Thanks, Mr Churchill,' I said. I stood up. The man was crazy! And I'd been crazy for taking the job.

But it was winter, and London was expensive, and I needed the money. I did not have the luxury of saying no to the radio man. So instead I stood up and made my excuses and fled the former First Lord of the Admiralty, and went into the common room instead. Hoping I could find the nurse.

Instead, I found myself.

3

'I'M ADOLF HITLER.'

'No, I'm Adolf Hitler!'

There were two of them, scrawny little f—kers with Charlie Chaplin moustaches, one an Irishman by his accent and the other a Jew, near as I could tell.

'Actually, *I'm* Adolf Hitler,' I said.

They both stopped what they were doing and glared at me in mutual pity. 'You? You don't even have a moustache.'

'Who does this guy think he is?' the Hitler on the left said.

'Maybe he thinks everyone can just be Adolf Hitler, eh?'

'Like you can just waltz right in!'

'He looks more like a Freud, or a Marx.'

'No, that's Freud over there.'

An old boy by the radio came slowly to life. 'I'm Albert Einstein!' he said, offended.

'Sorry, Al.'

'That's all right.' He settled back down again. I stared at them. I stared at them all.

'You are all insane!' I said.

Footsteps sounded behind me, high heels against the hard floor, and I could smell Chanel No. 5. All the inmates quieted down.

'What is going on here, please?'

She spoke English with a heavy accent. I turned and looked at her.

Her nails were long and sharp and painted a bright red colour. Her hair was blonde. Her eyes were blue and cold, and I was in love. She looked like she belonged with a whip in her hand, instead of the long syringe that she was holding. She wore a clean white smock and a murderous expression hidden behind a seemingly calm face. You can tell—you can always tell a killer. This woman was the real thing.

'Sorry, Nurse Beil.'

'Sorry, Nurse Beil.'

'We was just talking.'

She ignored the two Hitlers, and turned all the focus of her remarkable eyes on me.

'You're the new patient. Wolf.'

'Yes, Miss.'

'You will call me Nurse Beil.'

'Yes, Nurse Beil,' I said.

I could see why Lord Haw-Haw fell for her. I didn't know whether I wanted to kiss her or strangle her, or both. All I knew was that she had been too much woman for the British fascist to handle. Not me, though. I knew what women really wanted. I knew the violence that lay beneath their façade.

'You think you are Adolf Hitler? You? You are not worthy of mentioning that sacred man's name!'

So she was a National Socialist, too. I was a little surprised at that. My ideology had been popular once, but the communists had crushed my dreams of a unified Fatherland and my old comrades had either been killed or dispersed to all corners.

'I am here because I hope to get better, Nurse Beil,' I said, humbly. 'I did not mean to offend.'

'The *Führer*,' she said. 'He must be important to you.'

'Very, Nurse Beil.'

Her face softened. 'He led the way,' she said. 'His way can still be followed.'

'Followed?' I said.

She shook her head. 'Keep things quiet and you'll get no trouble here, Mr Wolf. But do not think to cross me.'

'No, Nurse Beil.'

She nodded.

'Good.' And with that she turned on her high heels and stalked off, rather in the manner of a panther patrolling its jungle domain. I stared at her backside in wonderment. She had the sort of magnificent ass that would have made even that old queen Ernst Röhm re-consider his sexual preferences.

'Don't even think about it,' Irish Hitler said, close in my ear.

'She's not for the likes of us,' the other Hitler said. 'This one has more pep in her than in a Daimler Double Six, if you know what I mean.'

'A Double Six? More like a Double D,' Irish Hitler said, and sniggered.

'Oh, shut the f—k up,' I said. On the radio, Ella Fitzgerald was singing "Let's Fall In Love". Albert Einstein stirred in his chair.

'Will you lot keep it quiet?' he said. 'I'm trying to figure out the wave-particle duality.'

No one paid him any attention. Nurse Beil vanished through the doors and the two Hitlers went back to arguing and playing cards.

I stood there staring after her.

So this was Miltraud Beil.

This was the woman I'd come to rob.

4

I'D THOUGHT IT would be easy to gain access to the nurse's office, but I was proven wrong. We were restricted to the main ward—our rooms and the common area—with supervised visits to the gardens when it wasn't raining. Everything else was out of bounds, kept behind locked doors and guarded over by the orderlies.

At first, it did not strike me as odd, for after all we *were* inmates in an insane asylum, but when I first ventured outside into the garden I was startled not only by the barbed wire over the high stone walls but by the sight of what appeared to be armed guards patrolling the building. I pointed this out to Winston Churchill (he insisted on the charade and, being forced to share a room with the awful man, I had little choice but to acquiesce to calling him that), and he nodded sagely.

'I told you,' he said, in a theatrical whisper. 'Not all is at it seems at Brookwood, my German friend.'

'I am not your friend.'

'Come, come, Mr Wolf. We have defecated together!'

He was referring to the time that I found myself trapped in the bathroom without realising he too was there. The strained sounds of Winston Churchill taking a dump still filled me with a horror I wished I could escape.

'I was only taking a piss,' I said, unconvincingly.

But I stared at the armed guards with a new uneasiness. Even a broken clock is right twice a day, and crazy people have a special sense of the absurd. They can tell when things are out of whack. Could Churchill be right?

But I dismissed the thought. There was no mystery, no *conspiracy* here. And my room-mate was no Winston Churchill. All I had to do was find some excuse into the nurse's office, steal the little box Lord Haw-Haw had told me about, and then discharge myself. There was a telephone available to the inmates for use and, once I had successfully accomplished my mission, all I had to do was ring him and I'd be released.

Or so he had assured me.

* * *

MY DAYS SETTLED into a leisurely routine. I would wake up, defecate (making sure Winston Churchill was nowhere in sight), then take breakfast with the others. They fed us well there, on the whole, with kippers and hard boiled eggs and toast and marmalade, and sausages on Tuesdays. Not a vegetable in sight, of course, this being England. An Englishman would not recognise a cucumber if you shoved it up his ass.

How I hated the English!

Of course I hated Jews, communists, homosexuals, Slavs, gypsies and Jehovah's Witnesses, too. How I hated Jehovah's Witnesses! And Freemasons, of course. And Negros. And the French. But then everyone hates the French. This hardly made me insane! In fact, I was the sanest man I knew.

I was certainly the sanest man in the Brookwood Insane Asylum.

Mornings and afternoons I spent playing chess or gin rummy with the others. We listened to the radio a lot. Musical Voyage, the Do Do Broadcasts, the Golden

Hour of Music, Vernon's All-Star Variety Concert and, of course, Lord Haw-Haw's Halftime Hour.

'Hello, Great Britain!' he would start. 'It's another scorcher of a day here in Luxembourg, where it is always sunny and the sky are always blue! You know, I often think of our current predicament—our refugee crisis, as I'm sure you'll all agree. Since the fall of mighty Germany into the hands of the dirty Jew communists, refugees from this once great nation have been flooding across Europe—nay, across the English Channel! And while we recognise certain brotherly affiliation with noble Deutschland, can our precious, small island take all these foreigners in? What of British jobs, for British people? What of the grand English tongue, assaulted—raped!—by the harsh vulgarity of German or, God forbid, Yiddish—for they all do come in, like rats, Jews and all. Our borders are must be protected, brothers! We must turn the tide of this human misery to protect our own, precious race, and the purity of our blood. Here's Fletcher Henderson with "Limehouse Blues".'

And the song would play, followed by a breathless testimonial for Bayer—Drugs You Can Trust.

Speaking of drugs, they did hand them out to the inmates as though they were sweets. Not Pervitin, of course—nothing to get you up and keep you going—but rather a lot of Veronal. It is a barbiturate made by Bayer, a sort of hypnotic. We were given the little pills three times a day by the nurses, who watched to ensure we took them. What I experienced was a mellow, relaxing, euphoric effect to the goofballs. After a few days I found myself having a rather pleasant conversation with Albert Einstein about rose gardening, and even conceded that perhaps some Jews were very nice people and most likely should not be terminated to preserve Aryan racial purity.

It was a nightmare!

It was Churchill, of all people, who put a stop to it.

'Listen, Wolf, or whatever your real name is–' he said.

'What's happening, Winston!' I said. I beamed at him as he leafed through a worn copy of Agatha Christine's *Appointment With Death*. He stared at me in disapproval.

'Don't you *see*, man?' he said. 'They're poisoning you! You have to stop taking the drugs.'

'How?' I said. 'They make sure to watch us take them.'

He smiled and opened his large palm. Inside it were three small pills.

'Like this,' he said.

He pretended to swallow the pills, then showed me how he palmed them.

'But they make me feel nice,' I said. 'I don't even feel angry anymore.'

'But you must be angry!' he said. 'The world isn't *nice*, Wolf. It is threatened every day by the forces of darkness, by violence, and hatred, and Fascism.'

'Benito Mussolini is a close personal friend of mine,' I told him.

'Listen to me! Keep your wits about you, fool. Or else…'

'Or else what?'

But he had settled down to a disgruntled mutter.

'Or else I don't know, Wolf. But I fear… I fear the worst. Not all is as it seems. Not with the world, and not here at Brookwood.'

I felt myself sober up. His tone had chilled me.

'But what do you mean?'

He shook his head.

'I pray,' he said soberly, 'we get out of here before you or I have occasion to find out.'

* * *

THAT DAY ON walking back from the Yiddish theatre, hidden in a crack in the fence, trapped in a pool of light, Shomer had found a flower growing. A tiny, blue Forget-Me-Not. He'd plucked it, carefully, gently, and cupped it in his hands. He carried it all the way home like a messenger with precious cargo. Fanya stood by the window and he came and wrapped his arms around her, and when she turned he showed her the flower, and for a moment there was something in her face that made him love her all over again, and all the more.

'I'd better put it in water,' she said.

Now he sits while they sleep all around him, his wife and children and the other families with whom they're forced to share this tiny space. Beyond the ghetto walls the German soldiers stand in wait. But in his mind he's free: as free as ever a man can be.

5

THE NEXT DAY I did as Churchill had advised me, and palmed the pills instead of swallowing. Nurse Beil watched me carefully, but I believed my sleight-of-hand had been successful.

Without the Veronal I found my old anger at the world return. With it came a new determination to end the case and get out of the madhouse. I had to get closer to Nurse Beil—I had to find a way into her office.

The day after that an altercation occurred in the common room. The two Hitlers had once again got into a shouting match, misquoting bits of *Mein Kampf* at each other and belittling each other's moustaches. I had tried to ignore them before, but this time, before anyone could intervene, the Hitlers' screaming match turned into a sudden fist fight, with much hair pulling and attempts at gouging eyes—they fought dirty, the scrappy little bastards.

The orderlies in white stormed into the common room and separated the fighters. In their wake came Nurse Beil. Her high heels echoed on the hard floor. She stood and watched the two Hitlers, each held in a Nelson by the orderlies. Both Hitlers were panting from the exertion, but the presence of Nurse Beil kept them quiet.

'You,' she said at last, pointing at the Hitler on the left, the one with the Irish accent. 'My office.'

'But Nurse—'

She gestured to the orderlies. 'Take him,' she said.

The orderlies dragged the mute Hitler away, and Nurse Beil turned on her heels and was gone.

* * *

THE HITLER NEVER came back. When I asked, I was told brusquely that he'd been moved to another facility. At first I didn't question it. But then, Albert Einstein disappeared.

6

CHURCHILL CORNERED ME by the showers.

'Did you hear?' he said. He opened the tap and cold water came streaming out.

'What are you doing?'

'Quiet!' he hissed. Or tried to. You can't really hiss that word. But still, he gave it a good try. 'We have to assume they're listening.'

'Heard what?' I said.

'Albert Einstein has disappeared.'

'You know he's not really Albert Einstein,' I said, tiredly.

He dismissed this with a wave of his podgy hand. 'I keep telling you, Wolf. Something's going on. Something bad.'

'Well, what do you want me to do about it!' I said.

'I worry I might be next,' he said. 'You're, what did you say you are? A confidential agent?'

'I prefer the term private eye,' I said.

'All these Americanisms!' he complained. 'Nevertheless.' He paced, back and forth.

'We need to investigate, Wolf.'

I didn't take it very seriously. But it occurred to me that I had been incarcerated in Brookwood for some time, and I was no closer to getting to my objective. The only way to make it to Nurse Beil's office, it seemed to me, was to come to her attention—to cause a ruckus, in other words. To make a *fuss*.

'Alright,' I said, having made my decision. 'But you'd have to play along.'

'Anything!' he said, looking relieved. 'What do you need me to do?'

'Only this,' I said. I balled my fingers to a fist.

'Wolf? What are you d—'

The air was knocked out of him with an awfully satisfying 'whoosh' as my fist sank into the fat folds of his soft stomach. Then I was on him. I had always wanted to beat the crap out of Winston Churchill.

'Wolf! Stop! For the love of—'

'Shut the f—k up, you degenerate!' I screamed, kicking him in the ribs, the stomach and the backside. He curled on the floor in a foetal position, his arms around his head, trying to protect it. He howled like a stuck pig. This was good. I had wanted to raise as much noise as possible.

In no time at all we had a circle of onlookers around us. The water in the shower had turned hot and steam was filling up the room. There was something so very satisfying about hurting Churchill. I had given in to the rage that I'd kept bottled up. Spittle flew from my lips and my shoes were covered in blood. Then the orderlies in white came and grabbed me. I fought them off. When I turned, I saw her approach.

Nurse Beil. She looked at the scene with calm contemplation. I just had time to admire her bosoms when one of the orderlies swung a truncheon. An awful black pain erupted in the back of my head, and as I fell to the floor, I saw Nurse Beil smile.

Then, for a long time, I saw and felt nothing.

7

'YOU HAVE BEEN a very naughty boy.'

There were heavy metal bars on the window and the sunlight coming through made her hair shine like gold. My head was sore and I needed a piss. I tried to tell her that but my mouth was gagged.

I tried to move, which was when I realised I was tied up in a chair.

'A very naughty boy,' she said, thoughtfully.

'Mmmmm-vvvv-ff!'

'You really *are* him,' she said, 'aren't you?'

'Mmmm-pff!'

'You're Adolf Hitler.'

She turned and looked at me. In her hand she held a syringe.

I stared at it. Her eyes were so empty and her lips were so full.

'Mmmmff!'

'No, don't speak,' she said. She moved towards me. She smelled of formaldehyde and Chanel.

'I used to listen to your speeches on the radio,' she said. 'About the fate of the Fatherland and how to solve the question of the Jewish problem. Things didn't really turn out the way we'd hoped, have they?' She straddled me and my breath caught. Her bosoms were close to my face and I could smell her sweat. I was suddenly as hard and as straight as the Berlin Victory Column. She wriggled in my lap and smiled. The tip of the syringe was right against my neck. I didn't know what was in it but my imagination had supplied the missing details.

Then she was rocking me, the yawning chasm of her feminine abyss grinding against my engorged excavator.

I couldn't breathe. The syringe was so very close and I thought of the men who had been called into Nurse Beil's office and never came back. But right then it didn't matter. I liked my women the way I liked my German shepherds: nasty and with sharp teeth.

When she climaxed I shuddered as my own vengeance weapon fired itself. My lap was a mess and the room smelled like chlorine and seawater. I felt her relax on top of me. For just a moment, the tip of the syringe had withdrawn from my neck.

I knew I only had one shot at it. Still painfully hard, I nevertheless made my move. My head drew back and then brought forth with as much power as I could summon. My forehead smashed into her nose and I could hear bones break. My knee rose and slammed into the entrance to her secret garden and she howled in rage and pain.

The chair crashed to the floor, Nurse Beil still on top of me, blood streaming from her face, the syringe still held in her hand. She raised it above me to stab.

'Die!'

I wriggled, trying to turn away. I realised the chair had broken in the fall. Suddenly, my hand was free. I held her wrist as she tried to stab me. She glared at me in frustration and pain.

'Die already!'

The syringe came down. It missed me by a hairbreadth and broke against the floor.

I grabbed the broken chair leg—and stabbed.

* * *

IT WAS OVER as quickly as it's happened. I remembered living with my niece, Geli, and how she'd used the opportunity of my business trip to Nuremberg to shoot herself with my pistol.

Women always betrayed me!

I released myself from the rope and stood, looking down at Nurse Beil.

I felt sad at this waste of German femininity. Nurse Beil would have made any Nazi proud. I saluted her.

Then I grabbed the little wooden box I'd been hired to find and it was time to make my escape.

8

THERE WAS ONLY one other door in her office and when I tried the handle it opened. I was tense, not knowing what to expect, worried that the sound of our scuffle may have drawn the guards.

The room was dark and very cold. I looked for a light switch, found it, and turned it on.

The corpses had been piled up neatly.

I saw the missing Hitler. His glassy eyes stared up at me over his sad little moustache. There were about seven corpses in the room, all in inmates clothing, all tagged with a label that was attached to their left big toe.

There was a desk in the room, laden with documents. I quickly looked through them. I saw references to "Special Treatment Centres" and "Action Group 4" and "Merciful Termination", and a letter from Oswald Mosley with the British Union of Fascists' lightning bolt, addressed to Nurse Beil, in which he commended her trial operational capabilities and asked when Phase Two of the programme could commence.

I stared at the letter.

I very much did not want to stick around for Phase Two.

There was another door in that room and I went through it. I discovered a large kiln, still warm to the touch: this must have been where they disposed of the corpses. I dismissed Mosley's methodology. Had I been in charge the system would have been far more efficient.

In any case, I didn't dally in the room. The next door led me outside.

I found myself in the garden. In the distance I could see the other inmates. I could also see the patrolling guards. Now I understood why they were there. This euthanasia of the mentally ill was a programme I myself had proposed back in Germany. Mosley was simply putting it into effect, trialling it here, perhaps in other parts of the island. No doubt they intended to extend it to small children, Jews and immigrants next. It had the sort of neat efficiency I could admire.

But right then I had to get out of the insane asylum.

I edged my way towards the gate. I hoped no one would see me. I dodged from bush to tree, trying to stay out of sight. Then I stumbled on a rock and fell face down into the grass.

Which was when the bloody bastards opened fire.

I screamed, 'Scheisse!'

The bullets hit the dirt beside me. I leaped to my

feet and began to run in a zigzag, trying to avoid the shots. In trying not to get hurt I ran towards the other inmates, hoping reasonably enough that they would serve as human shields.

Sensibly for them, they scattered.

'Wolf! Over here!'

It was Churchill. He was crouched behind a low rise of grass and was motioning to me frantically. I ran and took shelter with him.

'There's a breach in the wall over there,' he said, pointing. 'The masonry had caved in after the last rains. I was going to tell you. We can escape! The guards don't know it's there. We can get back to the outside world and warn them of the goings-on in this place!'

'Lead the way,' I said.

'There's nothing to it, old boy,' he said, and tried to smile bravely. 'We just have to make a run for it.'

And he took off like a big, fat hare.

There was, as he said, nothing to it. I followed suit, running behind him, as bullets zinged around us. We were almost at the wall, and I could see the breach ahead, where Churchill must have covered the small hole with sticks and leaves to hide it. I dove the last of the distance and landed hard—safely—against the wall.

'We did it, Winston! We did it!' I said, elated.

He plopped down beside me.

'Oh, Wolf,' he said. He tried to smile at me, but really it was a grimace of pain. I stared at Winston Churchill.

'Oh, dear.'

A small red flower bloomed on his breast. I thought back to my time in the trenches. The Great War. For a moment I was back there, gas shells whistling overhead. I grabbed the fat man. No man left behind. He was so heavy.

'No man left behind!'

I tried to pull at him. It was no use. And the guards were shouting as they came nearer. They'd have been on us in a moment.

He grabbed my shirt.

'You'll just have to go on… without me,' he said. 'Listen, Wolf. You must… fight on. Fight them on the beaches, fight them… in the fields and in the streets… never surrender!'

'What the *f—k* are you on about, man!' I screamed.

'Just… tell them. Tell them!'

And with that, his hand slackened its grip on me and fell by his side. I looked at him and realised I didn't even know his real name.

For all I knew, maybe he really *was* Winston Churchill.

I figured I'd never know. instead, I scrambled on hands and knees to the hole in the wall. I pushed away the leaves and branches and wriggled through just as the guards' footsteps sounded behind me. A couple of bullets pinged off the stonework but then I was through and on the other side.

For the first time in days, I drew in a breath of freedom.

It stank.

'Scheisse!' I said. 'What is that sm– oh.'

It really *was* s—t. I lost my balance and fell into the open cesspit.

'*Schiesse!*'

With faeces dripping down my face and clothes, I climbed out and began to clumsily run away from the insane asylum. The guards had wriggled through the hole, one by one, and began to fire, but I moved fast and their range was limited. I ran until I was in the shelter of a thick copse of trees. I made my way through the forest, found a stream and washed the effluence off of me as much as I could. I was finally free, if not yet out of danger.

At last, I made my way to a road. I stood on the side of the road and waited for a car. The first few, sensibly, drove right past me, but at last an old boy in a Bedford slowed down.

'Where you headed, son?' he said.

'London, sir.'

He looked at me quizzically.

'You're not one of them lunatics, are you?' he said. 'From up the road?'

'Oh, no, sir,' I said. 'Sane as they come, and twice on Sundays.'

'Well, hop on,' he said. 'I'm going as far as the Strand, as it happens.' He slicked back his hair. 'Got me a date tonight with a showgirl at the Adelphi.'

'Show*girl?*'

'Well, she was, once, old Margaret,' he said, with affection. 'And she still gives me the special rate. Hop on. You got a special someone, son?'

I thought of Miltraud Beil, and the way she lay there with the broken chair leg through her heart.

'Not at the moment, sir, no. Why do you ask?'

He beamed at me. 'It's St. Valentine's Day,' he said.

9

IT WAS COLD and on the way to London it had started to rain. I sat hunched in the back of the car, shivering. I wondered what it had all been for. I took out the little wooden box I'd taken from the dead nurse's office. What was so important to have cost me this much?

When I opened it all I found was a bundle of letters, tied in a string. I pulled it open and looked at them.

'*My dearest Gertraud, I want to cover your body in a thousand little kisses... your lips are as soft as the softest plums... Gertraud I long for your touch, every moment away from you is a misery I cannot bear to experience... Gertraud I adore you, dear girl!*'

'What utter f—king *trash!*' I screamed. No one heard me. 'I nearly died for, for... for *this?*'

Why were fascists always so floridly *sentimental!*

In a rage, I tore up the useless, stupid love letters and

tossed the shreds into the air. The wind snatched them and, in moments, they were gone.

I settled back against the cab, shivering, wet and cold, with tears of rage in my eyes. I hated them—hated them all! But mostly I hated what I'd become.

As we passed through Kingston-Upon-Thames, on the way into London, I saw a young boy and a young girl under the street light. He was holding a flower cupped in his hands and the girl was laughing and touching his face before she leaned in for a kiss. I only saw them for a moment.

Then the car went round a bend and they were gone.

THREE

THE LUNACY COMMISSION

Beyond the ghetto walls the trains pass in the night. They whistle greetings. Their wheels screech on the tracks. And Shomer's boy so loves the trains. Shomer and Avrom stand by the walls and listen. Shomer holds his boy's hand. There are rumours of the deportations to the East. Resettlement, some say. Others speak in hushed voices of more terrible things. The trains go full, but they return empty. And more and more they go.

There is nothing in fiction as terrible as that which can be found in life, this Shomer knows. Before the war he used to be a writer of shund; now his mind keeps desperately trying to escape.

'Daddy, daddy,' Avrom says. 'Can we go on the trains, one day?'

And Shomer doesn't have the words to say what can't be said. He hoists his boy up in his arms and holds him tight, and his mind shies from the glare. A story, then, another one. A simple, easy tale of mystery and murder in which order still prevails.

There's hope even in stories, still. As futile as they are. And so:

1

HIS NAME WAS Edward Kiss but despite the name he was as German as a liverwurst sandwich. He paced round my office above the Jew baker's shop and glared at me mournfully.

'You see, Herr Hitler, I fear someone wishes to murder me.'

I couldn't blame them if they would, I thought, but didn't say. I rubbed the bridge of my nose. The man was already giving me a headache and it wasn't even lunchtime.

'You must help me, Herr Wolf!'

It was a cold and dismal London spring and I had not seen the sun for days. I stared at this unwelcome specimen who had intruded into my office and wondered how I could get rid of him. Maybe with some lead aspirin, if I got lucky.

'What is it you do again?'

He puffed up all importantly. 'I'm an archaeologist,' he said.

'I see,' I said. I didn't.

'I am in London for a conference,' he said. 'Of the Ahnenerbe. We are a loosely-affiliated group of like-minded free thinkers on the origins of the Aryan race, racial theory, Glacial Cosmology, phrenology and the like. Important, real science. Not like that corrupted Jewish rot people subscribe to nowadays, that awful nonsense of relativity and suchlike.'

I was very fond of *Glazial-Kosmogonie* myself, though I didn't tell him that.

'So why would anyone want to murder you?'

He shrugged. 'I'm sure I don't know.'

'Do you owe anyone money?'

'I say, Herr Wolf!'

Which meant he probably did.

'Been rolling in the hay with the wrong *fräulein*, have you?'

'I say!'

Which meant he probably had.

'So what?' I said. 'What did you do?'

'Nothing, Her Wolf. I am the victim here!'

'Prospective victim,' I said.

'There have been two attempts so far,' he said. 'A highly-poisonous spider—a Chilean Recluse Spider, in fact–' he said it almost proudly, 'was on my pillow two nights ago on the ferry to England. I squashed it to a sludge. And yesterday afternoon while taking tea, I distinctly smelled the scent of garlic in my drink. Someone must have spiked it with arsenic. I spilt it immediately, of course.'

'These seem rather ridiculous ways of killing a man,' I said. 'I myself have always favoured the bullet to the head as the simplest solution.'

'Well,' he said. 'It is probably one of my colleagues. In our line of work we do sometimes tend to the theatrical.'

'A rival?'

'Perhaps. I am very highly regarded, you see. My research into the ancient Aryan-Atlantean culture of Tihuanaku was ground-breaking!'

'Was it really?'

'You *must* help me, Herr Wolf. Or next time they might succeed.'

'What is it you wish me to do, Herr Kiss?'

'Accompany me. Ensure my safety. I can pay you handsomely. Perhaps I did not mention I have a rather successful side-line as novelist. You must have heard of *The Queen of Atlantis*? Royalties from that and my other novels are robust.'

I myself had written one book, though it was non-fiction. It was about my struggle. Nowadays it was out of print, as National Socialism was no longer *de rigueur* in Europe. This was a source of some not-inconsiderable pain to me.

'I'm afraid I am more of a Karl May reader,' I said. 'Though I have recently become very fond of Agatha Christie.'

He huffed as though I'd offended him. 'Pish posh,' he said. 'My books explore the true heritage of the Aryan race as directly descended from the great civilization of Atlantis. It is a knowledge that will change everything we think we know about history!'

It sounded like the sort of s—t my old comrade,

Himmler, was always so fond of. But those days were gone forever. Once I was great, a leader of men. Now I worked cases out of a draughty office in Soho and I was lucky if I could pay the rent.

'So?' he said. 'Will you help me?'

I sighed and stared out of the window. I missed the sun, and my old summer pad in the Alps, and the dog I used to have.

'I will need the cash in advance,' I said.

2

A SMALL BANNER inside the lobby of the Midland Grand announced *The First Annual Ahnenerbe Conference on Race Science*. I noted with interest that the keynote speaker was to be none other than Hans F. K. Günther, the well-known eugenicist, whose books on the origin of race had formed much of my early thinking about the fate of the Fatherland and the problem of the Jewish Question. I would have liked to see him speak, but slapped across his face was the legend *Cancelled*.

Oh, well.

A much bigger sign above us said the conference was *Sponsored by IG Farben, purveyors of fine aspirin, heroin, toothpaste and pesticides*.

The hotel was next to King's Cross Station, where

they say that savage queen of theirs, Boudicca, lies buried. There was a woman who liked a bit of mass murder, I thought almost fondly. But she was nowhere to be seen. The hotel had a grand staircase with steps that looked threadbare, an army of servants that looked even worse, and dirty spittoons everywhere. Clearly it had seen better days and, it occurred to me then, so had I. Edward Kiss marched up to a reception desk set up in the lobby and announced his own arrival.

'Yes, yes, I am registered,' he said irritably to the woman in charge of handing out attendee badges. 'Kiss, Edward Kiss, surely you are familiar with my work in Tihuanaku—'

I heard the click of a cigarette lighter and smelled that foul smell of tobacco smoke. A cool, amused voice said, 'Ah, Herr Kiss.'

I turned and saw a hook-nosed blond with a full crown of hair, a deep tan, and a satisfied smirk wrapped around his cigarette holder.

My client stared at him in loathing.

'Beger,' he said.

'It is I. I have only recently returned from Tibet, you know. We did valuable work there, me and Schäfer.'

Kiss smirked right back at him. 'Measuring skulls? Counting bones? Fiddling with skeletons?'

'Valuable scientific work,' Beger said. 'Not something you'd know anything about, Kiss.'

'F—k you, Beger!'

'No thanks.'

The blond laughed. He too turned to the reception desk. 'Beger,' he said. 'But you know me, darling.'

The woman handing out badges almost blushed. Kiss fumed silently beside me.

But I had no eyes just then for either. Instead I stared appreciatively at Beger's companion. She stood there cool as a *gurkensalat* in winter, taking it all in and not giving anything back. She had dark hair, full breasts, a deep tan, and the sort of eyes that would make a *Schäferhund* s—t itself and get an erection at the same time.

'Who are you?' I said.

She gazed back at me coolly.

'Who the hell are *you*?' she said.

'Name's Wolf. I'm a private eye.'

'Like William Powell in *The Thin Man*?' She looked at me with amusement. 'Do you solve murders, too, Mr Wolf?'

'There is seldom any real mystery in murder,' I told her stiffly. 'I am far more curious to investigate *you*, Miss…?'

'Trautmann, if you must know,' she said. 'Erika Trautmann. I'm—'

'Let me guess. An archaeologist?'

'I study petroglyphs and rock runes, particularly in relation to the superior Aryan civilizations of prehistory.'

'Of course you do.'

'You do not believe us Aryans descended from a

superior race that first brought civilization to this world?'

'On the contrary,' I said, giving her my best smile. 'I believe it explicitly.'

'Good, then,' she said. Then she looked at me curiously. 'You remind me of someone,' she said. 'But I can't tell who.'

'I just have that kind of face,' I told her. 'I like yours more.'

She laughed. 'You think you're charming, don't you?' she said. But I could see that she liked it. I always could tell, you know.

'You will excuse us,' Beger said coolly. I doffed my hat to Erika Trautmann as the two of them headed towards the hotel's ballroom. By the desk, my client had finally gotten a nametag and turned to me with a scowl.

'Here,' he said. 'Your badge.'

'Oh.'

I put it on. It looked ridiculous.

'Well?' Kiss said. 'Shall we?'

I shrugged. 'It's your party.'

'It's my *life* that's at stake here!' he said.

'Don't worry,' I said as I followed him to the conference hall. 'You'll be as safe as Hildegard of Bingen's maidenhood.'

In that, of course, I was wrong.

3

A MAN FROM IG Farben opened the proceedings. I supposed he had every right—they had paid for it, after all. His name was Wilhelm Mann and he was a brutish looking c—t with close-cropped hair and the cold eyes of a pesticide salesman. He was the sort of guy who marries his cousin.

He spoke a few words—to scattered applause—then left the stage to the scientists.

The lectures were as boring as one could expect from a bunch of Germans who have fingered too many skulls in dark caves.

The material itself, though, was fascinating.

How the superior Aryan race evolved out of the ancient civilization of Atlantis, for which there was definitive proof in cave paintings uncovered by Altheim and Trautmann in France, for instance.

An old boy, Herbert Jankuhn, gave a rousing lecture on the mass execution of homosexuals in the ancient bogs of Tollund, of which he was very approving, and for which there was a loud round of applause.

Beger discussed his expedition to Tibet with the noted explorer, Ernst Schäfer, where they had indeed measured the skulls of the native Tibetans for comparison with modern-day Aryans, and also took samples of seeds.

It went on and on and I gorged myself on *spitzbuben* and butter cookies, of which I am very fond.

Then the conference finished for the day and the good Aryan professors and their assistants retired to the hotel bar, where they proceeded to get uproariously and disgustingly drunk. Watching them like this you could have thought the good old times of Weimar never ended, that we had never fought the good fight and lost to the communists in '33, that I had never fallen from grace and been imprisoned, and that National Socialism was still alive and well.

I hated them for that. For the truth was we *had* lost, and I had barely fled the Fatherland with my life, and the communists ruled Germany now. And I, who all of Germany knew and feared and loved at one time—I was a nobody now.

I hated them for that.

A flushed Erika Trautmann came up to me at some point and leaned in close. I could feel her heat, and smell the alcohol on her breath.

'You do not drink?' she said, only slightly slurring her words.

'I never drink,' I told her. 'It is a filthy habit.'

'A girl can be filthy,' she said, and gave me a leer. I felt my throat constrict.

'And you are so pure…' she said. 'Are you my Galahad?'

'Listen, Toots,' I said, 'all the knights are dead.'

Instead of an answer she reached quite boldly and grabbed me by the *fleischklößchen* without so much as a how-do-you-do. I gave a little yelp.

Sometimes this job was hard.

Something was getting hard, at any rate.

Her smile grew wider.

'Is that the Grail in your pocket?' she said, 'or are you just glad to see me?'

'Take your hands off of me!' I croaked. 'I do not like hussies, and besides I'm on the job.'

'F—k you, then!' she screamed in sudden fury, and tossed her olive martini in my face, the b—ch.

She stalked off. I massaged my groin and stared after her. It was funny, but I didn't think she was as drunk as she made herself out to be.

The man from IG Farben—Mann, I remembered his name was—circulated. I saw him speak to Kiss at some point, but they spoke quietly and only for a moment. At some point this Mann made to come up to me, but I avoided him easily. I do not like salesmen.

I kept an eye on Herr Doktor Kiss. He seemed to be having a marvellous time, though one incident did occur. At one point I noticed Kiss arguing loudly with a moustachioed man in his fifties.

'I have conclusively proven Atlantis, the cradle of Aryan civilization, was in the North Atlantic!' the man shouted, poking his finger in Kiss' chest.

'You fraud! You utter buffoon!' Kiss yelled, all but spitting in the other man's face in his passion. 'Your theory of the matriarchal society of ancient Atlantis is nothing but degenerate fetishism! Men ruled Atlantis, good Aryan men!'

'You imbecile!'

'Hack!'

'Gentlemen, enough!' I said, stepping between them. 'Herr Kiss, it is time to go.'

'F—k you, Wirth!' Kiss yelled, ignoring me as he tried to drunkenly launch himself at the other man. I held him back.

'Come,' I said; not entirely gently.

At last he relented. Last orders had anyway been called. Still yelling insults at this Wirth, he let me lead him away to his room.

I went in first and checked the room thoroughly, ensuring there were no silent assassins, exotic snakes or poisonous spiders under the pillows. The windows were closed shut and there was no one in the room.

'All right?' I said.

'Alright, Wolf,' he said.

I waited until he shut the door and locked it from the inside. I listened as he staggered round the room for a while, cursing Wirth and Beger and muttering about Atlantis. Then he finally plonked himself onto his bed and, moments later, began to snore.

Satisfied that I had done my job appropriately, I went to the adjacent room which Kiss had booked for me.

I fell asleep quickly, and was only woken up in the early dawn with heavy knocks on my door, to find two irate police constables who informed me Kiss had been murdered.

4

'WHAT THE BLOODY hell do you mean, murdered?' I said. 'He was sleeping like a baby last I checked.'

'Baby's dead,' Constable Marsh said.

'Bye bye, baby,' Constable Carr said mournfully.

'Know anything about that?' Constable Marsh said.

'Me?' I said. 'I didn't do it! He hired me to protect him!'

'Good at your job, then, are you?' Constable Carr said.

'Look,' I said, 'what is all this about? Are you sure he's dead? It makes no sense.'

'See for yourself.'

'Yeah.'

'Come along then, Wolf, or whatever you call yourself.'

'Yeah.'

I followed them out to the corridor. The door to Kiss' room was open now, broken by the police from the outside. I stepped into the room and saw Kiss curled on the armchair in a frozen pose, his nails torn and his face caught in a frightening rictus, as though whatever he'd seen in his last ever dream so spooked him that he died there and then.

Oh, he was *dead*, there was no doubt about it. He was dead as a doorknob. He was dead as a dodo. He was dead as whatever stupid f—king expression the English have for this sort of thing, in that filthy inbred tongue of theirs.

He was very f—king dead, is what I'm saying.

The only thing I couldn't work out was *how*.

'The door was locked,' I said dumbly. 'From the *inside*.'

'Yes, yes,' Carr said. 'It's a real mystery.'

'Quite a conundrum,' Marsh said.

'The windows are closed!' I said. I sniffed the air. He'd soiled himself in death. It smelled disgusting. Something else, too, very faint now. Something like vanilla or almonds.

'Maybe he killed *himself*,' Carr said.

'Suicide, for sure,' Marsh said, nodding sagely. 'Looks like a clear suicide to me.'

'Either way who gives a s—t for one dead kraut,' Carr said, and glared at me as though hoping I'd be next.

'What?' I said. 'You can't just *leave* it!'

'The hotel wants the room,' Marsh said.

'They'd like the corpse *out*,' Carr said.

'And *we'd* like a bacon batty and a hot cuppa,' Marsh said.

'You're s—t for protection,' Carr said.

'S—t,' Marsh said, nodding.

'Now f—k off,' Carr said. 'Or we'll book you for murder, or obstruction, or for being a German in the wrong place at the wrong time.'

'Yeah,' Marsh said, 'the wrong place being England, and the wrong time being right now.'

'F–' I started, then stopped when I saw them reaching for their batons.

I stared at my former client. Kiss was dead and that was that. I'd done my best for him, but sometimes your best is just not enough, and what were you going to do?

'Scram,' Carr said.

So I scrammed.

5

'WHAT IS THE meaning of this?' Herman Wirth said. He was the moustachioed man I had seen arguing with my client the night before.

'Kiss is dead,' I said. 'One of you lot must have murdered him.'

'Murdered!' He stared at me in wounded surprise. His moustache quivered. 'That's absurd.'

They were gathered in the lobby, these scientists of the fallen Reich that never came to be, these eugenicists and race theorists and archaeologists of ancient Mu or Atlantis, or wherever it was they said the Aryan stock came from. They looked up to me, I realised at that moment. It had been a long time since anyone had looked at me that way. Once, I had been their leader. Back then, I still had my moustache. Then came the Fall; the communists took power; the Reichstag burned and I was tossed into a concentration camp, and barely escaped with my life; to England; to this dismal s—t hole of a place.

Now they no longer even remembered me. I, who was once their master!

'Anyway,' I said, 'it's none of my business, and the police are saying it's suicide.'

They visibly relaxed. And I knew then that one or more of them had killed him. I just didn't know how—or why.

A familiar fury took hold of me then. Back when I was a leader of men, all of Germany marched to the beat of my drum. I would stand on the podium and preach National Socialism and they lapped it all up—they loved me for it. I could not *abide* to be dismissed!

It came down to *order*. There had to be order, above all things.

'But it was not,' I said then. 'One of you *is* guilty. I can smell it on you, like a bad sweat. And I *will* find you.'

'You're not even a guest here,' Wirth said. 'I demand you leave immediately!'

'Actually...' This from Beger, the tanned blond. 'Herr Wolf is a registered member of the conference.' He smirked at the assembly. 'I believe he has just as much right to be here as any of us.'

I realised he was right, of course. But still. I was a foreigner in this country where they did not like foreigners, and while these scientists would leave London in a matter of days, I would remain behind, and I knew how the police here treated the German refugees. We were little more than rats to them. The sensible thing was to depart, and keep the client's money…

'I would like to speak to each of you in person,' I said.

'Who does he think he is, Hercule Poirot?' I heard someone mutter. I ignored it. I would not be compared to a f—king *Belgian*!

'Beginning with *you*, my dear,' I said.

Erika Trautmann turned and gave me an icy smile. 'You'd have to buy me a drink first,' she said.

'That could be arranged.'

'Then lead the way, Herr Wolf. And I will have the *expensive* champagne.'

I thought of poor old Kiss' money in my pocket and just shrugged as I led her to the bar.

6

'DID YOU KNOW him well?'

She sipped from her coupe glass. 'Everyone knew Edward. He was a pompous s—t but, you know. We're all one big happy family.'

'The *Ahnenerbe*,' I said.

'Yes. There has been talk of establishing a permanent institution, you see, but that rather fell by the wayside when the communists took over. Some of us still believe in Nazism, though. Science proves it. Germans are pure of blood, Jews and Gypsies are inferior races. It's there in the runes on the cave walls, if you know where to look. Besides, Kiss was always happy to buy a girl a drink.' She drowned her glass and waved it at the bartender for another.

'So you had no reason to dislike him?'

She shrugged. 'I'm just a girl,' she said. 'Listen, Wolf, or whatever you call yourself. Kiss was a passable novelist and a mediocre archaeologist. If that's a reason to kill someone half the people here would be dead already.'

'I saw him shouting at that fellow, Wirth, last night,' I said.

'Ah, Herman,' she said. 'He is our co-founder. Joined the Party early, you know. Big admirer of Hitler—that's who you remind me of! Only he had a moustache… Anyhow, Herman's paper on "The Prehistory of the Atlantic Nordic Race" was very important work. But he and Kiss did not see eye to eye.'

'Oh?'

She shrugged again. The bartender poured her another glass of overpriced champagne. 'Herman thought the ancient Atlantids worshipped a single god, and were ruled by women. Kiss has—had, I mean—other ideas. But people don't die over scientific arguments, Herr Wolf.'

'No,' I said. 'They die over a lot less.'

I stared at her over her glass. Something rang false about Miss Trautmann.

'Where are you based?' I said.

'The Netherlands, nowadays. Most of us had to leave Germany, you see. But we carry on the work.'

'You travel much?'

She smiled. 'It is my work. We all do. I had only recently come back from the Middle East, as it happens.'

'Alone?'

'With Franz Altheim.' She looked at me coolly. 'He is one of my lovers. Do I shock you?'

'Lady,' I said, 'very little shocks me.'

She sipped her drink. 'Are we done here?'

'What were you doing in the Middle East?'

'Studied the pyramids and inscriptions in Abu Simbel. That sort of thing.'

'And did you arrive at any conclusions?'

'Yes,' she said. 'It's too hot there and the food's unbearable.' She laughed throatily and pushed closer into me. Her knee pushed between my legs and rubbed against me. 'Can't find a decent bratwurst *anywhere*, if you know what I mean.'

The woman was insufferable!

'Thank you, Miss Trautmann,' I said stiffly (in more ways than one), and got up. 'That will be all for now.'

'I'm in room 405, if you need to ask me any more… questions,' she said.

'But that's the room next to Kiss'!' I said, surprised. 'Did you hear anything in the night?'

'I'm afraid not,' she said. 'I'm a heavy sleeper.'

She downed the second glass and sauntered away,

glancing back at me only once. She didn't look like a killer but then again, those kind of dames never do.

7

'KISS?' HERMAN WIRTH said. 'The man was a fool but I didn't kill him. If I went around blithely murdering every idiot who called himself an archaeologist there'd be no one left at the Ahnenerbe.' He grimaced a smile at me and helped himself to some nuts on the bar.

'What did you disagree about?'

'What didn't we,' he said, chewing loudly. The man was a pig. 'You can come hear my talk on ancient Atlantis and make up your own mind. It is most illuminating.'

'I'm sure it is.'

'Listen, my friend,' he said, leaning close and spitting bits of nuts in my face. '*Cherchez la femme*, do you get my meaning?'

'I'm not sure that I do.'

'Kiss had a thing for the Trautmann woman. Well, you saw her. She's quite the piece. My colleagues all f—k each other like dogs in heat, you know.'

'I didn't. Are you suggesting Kiss and Trautmann had an affair?'

'I'm sure I couldn't say.'

'Why would she kill him?'

'Listen, man,' he said. 'What does it matter who killed him, when you don't even know *how* it was done? I understand the room was locked from the inside.'

'It's a mystery,' I admitted. I hated mysteries.

'Must have killed himself, then,' Wirth said. 'And good riddance.'

'You just suggested Trautmann killed him.'

'Did I?' He wiped his lips with a napkin and stood up. 'Well, you're the detective, Herr Wolf. You figure it out. Pip-pip, tra la la!' He saluted me and sauntered off.

I tried to figure out my next move when the man from IG Farben—the one who looked like he married his cousin—came up to me. Today he was in a conservative grey suit. He shook my hand and looked at me gravely.

'Wilhelm Rudolf Mann,' he said. 'International sales. At your service.'

'Are you?' I said. 'At my service?'

'Not really,' he said. 'Herr Wolf, we at IG Farben do not like a spectacle. Slow and steady and respectable, that's more us. So as regrettable as Herr… Kiss, was it? Kiss' death is, the case's closed. There *is* no investigation. And we'd much rather you just… moved on. Do you get my meaning?'

'Scram?' I said.

He looked at me dubiously. 'Yes, that,' he said.

'I'm afraid I cannot. I still have principles.'

'You are a buffoon!' he said. 'I know who you are, who

you once were, at any rate. I believed in the cause. I'd joined the Party back in '31, you know. I was a Brownshirt, too. I was as good a Nazi as anyone here.'

'Mazel tov,' I said.

He looked at me in anger. 'But you are being bad for *business*,' he said. 'Walk away, Herr... *Wolf*. Go back to your office in Berwick Street—'

He made a point of telling me he knew where I lived—

'And find some other employment. A juicy divorce, perhaps?'

'I don't work divorces,' I told him, angry. Though of course he was right. You had to pay the rent *some*how.

'Word to the wise, Herr Wolf. Walk away.'

And with that he turned and left me there, full of thought.

8

'YOU'RE BARKING UP the wrong tree, Wolf, old boy,' Bruno Beger said. He looked at me pleasantly and drank his beer. 'Kiss wasn't anybody.'

'He was your rival.'

'Hardly! He was a fantasist and his best days were behind him. Must be why he topped himself.'

'It was murder.'

'Not what the police are saying.'

'Listen, Beger. British cops don't give two f—ks about

a dead German. Not these days. What surprises me is that neither do any of you.'

'What can I tell you, Wolf. He wasn't the most popular guy.'

'Did you kill him?'

He laughed in my face. 'Are you that inept?' he said. '*This* is how you go about solving crime, randomly accusing people?'

I shrugged. Truth was I just wanted to see his reaction. I said, 'Where were you last night?'

'I had a few drinks, then went back to my room.'

'Were you alone?'

He smirked and didn't answer.

'Who do you work for, really?' I said.

'I'm just an anthropologist.'

I let him go, at that. They were all liars; scam artists who preached Aryan superiority and Atlantis while doing… what?

It had not escaped me that these people, in the guise of harmless scientists, could travel freely—and did so. That they could go places others could not. And moreover, could gather information while doing so.

There was a word for that, and the word was *spies*.

They were all former Nazis—devoted ones. But National Socialism had collapsed with my Fall. My former comrades had dispersed to all corners. I knew Hess was in London, though I had not seen him in over two years. Goering had wormed his way into the good graces of the communists and now served in some function back in Germany—the fat c—t always knew how to sail with the wind. The others I knew little about and cared even less. They had betrayed me—they had all betrayed me!

I should have ruled Germany—I should have ruled the *world*!

But anyway.

If these people were spies—then who did they work for?

I settled my by now considerable bar tab and made my way back up the stairs to Kiss' room. The police had come and gone and the broken door remained hanging open, so I stepped in. The corpse had been removed but no attempt had been made to clean up the room.

I looked around. There were signs of a struggle, but I knew Kiss was alone. Something had spooked him, inside the room. I saw the expression on his face in death. He must have moved around, tried to escape his fate somehow. The chair was broken and he had thrashed and flailed before death took him.

How did he die?

I searched the room—

There.

Some fine powder on the floor under the air vents. I didn't touch it. I knelt down, though my knees creaked, and sniffed. Kiss had been right. The killer or killers were theatrical. I did not like the theatre, myself.

You see, this is what these f—kers never understand. Murder is not an elaborate *show*. It takes no costumes, sleight of hand, exotic reptiles or fireworks. Murder is utilitarian and simple and brutal and it's too f—king *easy*. You don't need brains to kill a man. You just need to be willing to blow their brains out.

Murder, truly, is the triumph of the will.

I looked around some more. I noted someone had gone through the stuff before me. Kiss' suitcase, previously close, was open on the bed. It had been tossed. It did not surprise me.

Very few things did, these days.

Kiss had flashed his cash around. I did know that— the man paid me fully in advance.

He said he had independent income from his novels.

But in my experience no one earned as badly as a writer. You may as well try to sell scotch eggs to the French or good wine to the English. There's just no future in it.

So had Kiss lied to me?

And if so, where did he get his money?

9

'YOU MAY BE wondering why I'd gathered you all here,' I said.

I'd always wanted to say that.

Erika Trautmann took a sip of wine and smiled at me sweetly. 'Not really,' she said.

Beside her were Bruno Beger, the blond anthropologist; Herman Wirth, the moustachioed Atlantis aficionado; and Wilhelm Rudolf Mann, the sales agent from IG Farben.

'Get on with it, then,' Wirth muttered. He lit a cigar.

Beger smiled as he lit a slim cigarette. 'Let the man speak, Herman,' he said.

Mann said nothing, just glared.

I sighed.

'Very well,' I said. 'One of your comrades, Edward Kiss, has been murdered in this very hotel. None of you seem concerned in the slightest.'

'He was a s—t,' Wirth said.

'He was not a very good archaeologist, I'm afraid,' Beger said; almost apologetically.

'He was an inadequate lover,' Erika Trautmann said. Then: 'What?' into our expectant faces.

I sighed again. I could feel a headache coming on.

'Yet one of you felt strongly enough about the man to commit murder.'

'Absurd, man!' Wirth said.

Beger just laughed. The Trautmann woman sipped her wine. The man from IG Farben glared wordlessly.

'The problem with amateurs,' I said, 'is that they make things needlessly complicated. In this case, a real locked room mystery. How *did* they do it? Was it the snake on the bell cord? Was it bullets made of ice? Was some sort of specially-trained pygmy assassin hidden behind the curtains? This is all nonsense.'

'I told you it is,' the man from IG Farben said. 'So why are you still here?'

'You!' I said, pointing. 'What does IG Farben sell, Herr Mann? Fine toothpaste, for sure. Aspirin, and heroin of the highest quality, indubitably. But something else, too.'

'Yes?'

'Yes,' I said. 'Pesticide. Zyklon B, to be exact. Hydrogen cyanide, which comes conveniently prepared in capsule form. The very poison gas that *your* company manufactures!'

'So? Anyone can buy that at their convenience,' he said. 'I hardly carry pesticide around with me, Herr Wolf.'

But I had already dismissed him.

'You!' I said, pointing to Erika Trautmann. 'It was *your* room that was directly adjacent to Herr Kiss'. The poison was administered through the connecting air vents. The pellets were simply dropped through. On exposure to air the gas was released. Herr Kiss had less than two minutes to live. He died in agony upon inhaling the gas.'

I looked at them triumphantly.

They stared back at me with indifference. Beger took a drag on his cigarette. Trautmann sipped her wine. Mann and Wirth scowled.

'Are you accusing me?' Trautmann said.

'You!' I said, pointing to Beger. I was beginning to enjoy myself. 'You said you had spent the night in your room, with company. I suggest to you that the reason you were not alone was that you spent the night with Miss Trautmann!'

'So?' Beger said. Trautmann smirked. 'I am very fond of Erika and, besides, she's a tiger in the sack.'

'You're not too bad yourself,' she murmured.

'If Miss Trautmann wasn't in her room, it was easy enough for someone else to gain entrance and administer the poison across,' I said.

'So I'm not guilty?' she turned those innocent eyes on me and pouted, almost as though I'd disappointed her.

'Which leaves *you*,' I said softly.

'I beg your pardon?' Herman Wirth said, looking startled, and not at all pleased.

'This is *your* little operation, is it not?' I said. 'The Ahnenerbe. A think tank, I believe you call it. An odd assortment of Nazi-sympathetic scientists, archaeologists and the like. You could have been a real somebody, if the Party had won in '33. But with the communists in charge, you are diminished. The world laughs at your science. They embrace *Jew* science—Freud and Einstein! Relativity, psychoanalysis! They laugh at your stories of Atlantis! It must hurt, Herr Wirth. It must hurt so bad, to lose.'

'Why would I kill Kiss?' he said. 'You are being ridiculous.'

'My guess is he was blackmailing you,' I said. 'He had too much money for an archaeologist. What he had on you I don't know. It's always something grubby and sordid, though. Proof of an affair or embezzlement, maybe a compromising photograph or two. This is what you people never understand. Murder is a *simple* art.'

'Stay back,' he said. I saw then the gun he had in his lap. It was pointing at me. 'You can't prove any of this, Wolf, or whatever you call yourself. You're a nobody.'

'Take it easy with that gun,' I said.

'The man was a fool! His research was laughable. It threatened the integrity of my work.'

'Is that why you killed him?'

He all but gloated. 'It was simple enough,' he said. 'Zyklon B, why had no one else thought of this? I gassed the f—ker and didn't feel a thing. You know, we could have got rid of the Jews this way, and IG Farben would have made a fortune in the process selling the stuff.'

'Why did you kill him?'

'There was a night in Tangier, we both got very drunk and spent the night with some Moroccan houris. You know how it is. The man must have had a camera on him. When I came to he had all he needed. I am not a rich man, Herr Wolf. The goal of my life is science, not filthy lucre. I had no choice. You *must* see that.'

Beger tapped out his cigarette. 'Put the gun away already, Herman,' he said irritably. 'Herr Wolf was just leaving.'

'Was I?' I said.

'Yes. This charade has gone on long enough. What do you expect to happen now, Wolf? The case is closed and the police aren't interested. No one gives a s—t.'

'Yeah,' Erika Trautmann said, and drained the last of her drink. She stared me at through the glass. 'You're boring us,' she complained.

I stared pleadingly at the man from IG Farben, but he seemed lost in thought.

'Mass gassing?' he said. 'How would that work? You'd have to brick the windows and lock the doors, drop the pellets in through the air vents... Yes, it could work, I suppose, on an industrial scale. But you'd need the infrastructure! Camps, trains to bring them all there... Crematoriums for after the fact...'

He was lost in what must have been, for him, a pleasant daydream.

'Well?' Wirth said. The gun was still pointing at me.

I stared at him in loathing.

I had found the killer and solved the crime.

And it had made no difference at all.

That's the thing about crime. Bad deeds often go unpunished. The guilty walk free. It doesn't matter if you find the killer if there is no one left to keep the law. All that bull the Dickson Carrs and Allinghams of the world try to sell you don't mean s—t in the final count.

Murder's just another dirty business.

'Tons of Zyklon B...' Mann said, dreamily.

Wirth smiled at me nastily. The gun was pointing at my abdomen.

'Well?' he said. 'Scram.'

So I scrammed.

* * *

THEY RETURN HOME and Shomer tacks Avrom into bed, beside his sister. He sits there by the window and watches his children sleep. Beyond the ghetto walls the trains pass, whistling, going east. The night's as quiet as it ever can be, here. The single candle's light ebbs against the walls. And Shomer closes his eyes, and wishes he could sleep. How softly do the children breathe.

They have that, he thinks. For as long as they have breath, they will—

FOUR

A WONDERFUL TIME

I n another time and place Shomer stands with his back
to the wall of the ghetto. He turns the precious postcard
over and over in his hands.

"Having a wonderful time", it says, and nothing more—
nor can it, for even the mere arrival of this missive from
the outside is a miracle. It is signed Betsheba, and hidden
in its bland exterior—a picture of Niagra Falls, in distant America beyond the seas—is a world of meaning. For
she has made it, Fanya's sister, she has escaped the war in
Europe and the murder of the Jews and she is in America,
she is safe, she's free.

And Shomer marvels: how a small rectangle of paper
can offer so much hope. He will take it home and show
his wife, and they will celebrate. For himself he has no
more concern: if only he could get out Fanya and the
children...

But the ghetto is encircled by the German soldiers, and

more and more the trains come to the Umschlagplatz*: they depart laden with Jews and they return empty. And more and more they come.*

And Shomer hides the postcard on his person, and he measures out his steps like a prisoner in the prison yard. For he does not yet know how much time they have left.

Only his mind is free, and in his mind, as always, he constructs a story, a cheap and nasty tale. For only in his fantasy can he escape this time and place.

1

THE POSTCARD SAID, "Having a wonderful time." I turned it over and over in my hands. It was addressed to me in a girlish hand. The address read, "Herr Wolf, Detektiv. Above the Jew baker shop, Berwick Street, London."

It was dated 15 March, 1938. It was a month out of date.

'You don't look much like a detective,' the policeman said. His partner sniggered. I could smell fresh bread from the bakery downstairs, and *Kaiserschmarrn mit apfelkompott*, a Bavarian specialty—it is like a rich torn pancake served with apple sauce. It made my stomach rumble. I had always loved sweet things.

I swept my hand across the bare office. 'I have a desk and two chairs, one for visitors, a hat stand and a type-writer–' I said, then gave up. The typewriter was out of ink, anyway, and only my hat hung on the hat stand. It was a nice hat. A fedora. It was a little beat-up by life, just as I was. But it was still hanging.

'Who is it from?' I said.

'This is what we hoped you would tell us,' the policeman said. His name was Redgrave.

'And since when do the fuzz deliver the mail?'

They looked at each other, then looked at me.

'What?' I said. I had a sudden bad feeling about all this. 'I don't know nothing.'

'Do you not,' the other policeman, Lockwood, said.

'Says he doesn't,' Redgrave said.

'You believe him?' Lockwood said.

'Seems a trustworthy sort,' Redgrave said, and they both chuckled. Then Lockwood dangled handcuffs at me with his index finger.

'We'd like you to come with us, Mr Wolf.'

'But I didn't do nothing, I told you!'

'Come, come, Mr Wolf.'

Redgrave's hand went to his night stick and stayed there. I gave up.

But I was most certainly not having a wonderful time.

2.

THERE'S A CERTAIN righteous cruelty in the face of your typical Bavarian schoolmistress: as though she had seen everything in the world and found nothing but disappointment, yet was still determined to carry out her duty. It was the sort of face to put fear into old men and young boys alike. There was just one small thing: she was dead.

In death she looked equally disappointed—as though when the big moment finally came it was nothing but a let-down. I'd seen people die before and helped a few more on their way, but that kind of a death mask was new to me.

I said, 'I don't know her.' I stared some more. That face, there was something about it, like a horse one once rode in somebody else's stables.

'You sure, gumshoe?'

I nodded, slowly.

'Then why was she carrying a postcard addressed to you in the pocket of her coat?' Redgrave said.

It was a not unreasonable question.

I'd been wondering the same thing myself.

'Where did you find her?' I said.

'Tossed in the back of the picture house on Shaftesbury Avenue,' he said, 'by the bins.'

'The Avenue Pavilion?' I said. I knew the cinema vaguely.

He nodded.

'And with a .43 in the back of her head.'

'Nasty.'

Execution style, I thought. Neat and professional. I liked things neat. And I appreciated a professional.

'German?'

'Refugee, probably,' Redgrave said, with a little dis-
taste in his voice.

'Illegal, most likely,' Lockwood said. He shrugged.
'Not much we can do, then, I suppose,' he said.

'What do you mean?' I said. 'This is a murder!'

He just shrugged again. 'Do you know how many of
you there are now?' he said.

'Too many,' his partner said.

'Coming over here, like rats from a drowning ship.'

'*Germans*,' Redgrave said, with loathing.

'Illegals. More and more of you each day. Well, we did
the best we could.'

'Best we could.'

'If we were going to arrest anyone, it would probably
be you.'

'Me?' I said. 'But I didn't *do* anything!'

'Oh,' he said. 'But I'm sure you have, Mr Wolf.' He
looked at me, almost curiously. 'Didn't you use to be
somebody, once?'

I had nothing to say to that. He smiled, thinly, and
covered the woman's face.

'You can go,' he said.

And that was that.

3

BACK IN 1923, briefly, I had been somebody. Standing

in the huge hall of the Bürgerbräukeller in Munich, with the smell of spilled beer and damp coats and cheap cigars and women's perfume, I gave a speech. I had been good at giving speeches. There had been an anger then in Germany that was palpable, as thick in the air as the fug of cigarette smoke is during Oktoberfest. Girls in dirndls served the patrons, and giant swastika flags hung from the walls under the glass chandeliers. I told my audience that Germany was suffering. That Germany needed saving. That the Jews were the cancer and that I was the cure.

Oh, they cheered. How they cheered! It was time, I told them. It was time to take back *control!*

They loved it. They lapped it all up.

Then we marched on the Odeonsplatz and everything went to s—t. Someone shot Max Scheubner-Richter through the lungs and the fucker fell and, since we had linked our arms together, he brought me down with him. I'd dislocated my shoulder and was in quite great pain. I almost wished he came back to life just so I could shoot him myself.

After the fire fight I ran. We had a getaway car but it broke down on the way to the Alps and so instead I headed to this little village called Uffing, on the shores of the Staffelsee. It is a very pretty place.

* * *

I STARED AT the postcard in my hands now. The two police officers had left it with me. Neither snow, nor rain, nor heat, nor gloom of night stayed these couriers from the swift completion of their appointed rounds. As Herodotus would have said.

The postcard showed a view I knew well. It was the Staffelsee.

It is a charming lake. I had once gone boating there in the summer. It had been a beautiful sunny day. But back in 1923 I made my way there in the dark, and at last knocked on the door of the Hanfstaengls' house in Uffing. The money grabbing Hanfstaengls, some called them. Putzi and Helene. Putzi had been with me in Munich, but he ran just as soon as trouble started. He'd be halfway to Austria by now, and snorting Pervitin in Piesendorf before the night was out.

Helene opened the door.

By God but there was a woman! She had the sort of legs you could suck for popsicles and the bush of a French prostitute. She was American, but of good Aryan stock. What she was doing married to a Hanfstaengl was anybody's guess.

'Adolf?' she said. Her hand rose to her mouth—too theatrically, I thought. You know those hausfraus and their flair for amateur dramatics. 'I heard the news on the wireless, is Putzi—'

'Putzi's fine,' I said—cursing him inwardly. 'He should be halfway across the Alps by now. I would be too if it weren't for the d—n Maybach breaking down.'

'You poor thing,' she said. She ushered me in. 'You're wounded!' she said.

'I bleed for Germany,' I told her.

'Oh, Adolf!'

She busied herself around me like a bitch in heat. I could smell the foliage of her garden getting all moist.

I knew she wanted me. Women always did, back then, you see.

I let her minister to me.

. . .

Later, the G-d d—ned village policeman came to arrest me.

4

'THAT'S IT!' I said.

Two pigeons flew away, startled, and an old homeless woman, pushing a cart filled with dirty clothes, leered at me.

'What's it, ducky?' she said. 'Come give old Mildred a kiss.'

She stuck her tongue out at me through broken black teeth.

'Get away from me, you filthy whore!'

Old Mildred lifted her skirt at me and leered some more. There were broken red veins in her nose. I tried not to look at what was under the skirt. 'You'll come around, ducky,' she said. 'Sooner or later, they all do.'

I shuddered and walked away. I knew who the dead

woman was after all, I realised. Anna or Marta, one of those names. She had been the Hanfstaengls' maid back in Uffing.

How she turned up dead, in London, and with my name on her person, I had no idea.

It really wasn't my business to get involved in. I wasn't getting paid. Though someone must have had a reason to off the old woman, and in London, in this cold year of our lord 1938, that reason was more often than not hard, cold money.

People died just as much from the simple reason of being a foreigner, of course. But that usually involved a beating, not an execution.

'Schiesse!' I said, to no one in particular. A pigeon came and landed by my feet and stared up at me with the dispassionate gaze of an SS Rottenführer.

I was out of work and I was out of luck and I was going to take on this s—t show of a case, just on the off chance there was something in it for me.

* * *

IT TOOK ME three tries and on the fourth I struck lucky. I'd gone through Soho, to those boarding houses I knew where they hired out rooms to foreigners. I passed a shop with a sign that said, 'No Germans, No Dogs.' On the wall I saw a poster of my old friend, Oswald Mosley, the leader of the British Union of Fascists. He had a thin moustache and a mouth like a smiling rat's.

I'd heard he was going to run for Prime Minister and, if so, rumour was he might just get in.

The last boarding house was on Greek Street. It was ran by a Madame Blavatsky—not the one who talked to ghosts, though she claimed to be a distant relation. I had run into this Blavatsky on a previous case. Now she glared at me suspiciously from behind her tea service.

'You again? What do you want?'

'It's nice to see you too,' I said. 'Nice weather we're having, what?'

'What?'

'What?'

'I *said*, nice weather we're—oh, forget it,' I said. 'Listen to me, you old crone, I'm looking for a woman who might have been staying here. Bavarian, late fifties. As ugly as a bulldog and twice as vicious, at a guess.'

'Anna Maria Fischer,' Madame Blavatsky said. I was a little taken aback.

'Really?'

'Found her, didn't they,' she said. 'Knew it had to be her. Someone stuck a bullet in that gob of hers. She still owes me two weeks' rent.' She looked at me with mournful eyes. 'Who's gonna pay me now, Wolf?'

'Don't look at me,' I said. 'I haven't a farthing to my name.'

'Listen you f—king kraut,' she said. 'You wouldn't be here at all if you didn't think there was something in it for you down the road. So I'll tell you what. You can go up and rummage through her knickers drawer to your heart's content, but if you find any money later on along the way you bring it here, you savvy?'

'You'd trust me to do that?' I said.

She shrugged, lifted a dainty foot and farted. 'Got nothing to lose, have I,' she said.

She reached for the radio and twiddled the knob until the Lord Haw-Haw Half-Time Show came on. He was spouting off as usual.

'England for the English! For too long have we lived under the yoke of Europe on our doorstep, the encroachment of foreigners onto our sacred soil! No more! It is time to take back con—and now for a word from our sponsor.'

I left her there and went up the stairs as angelic trumpets played on the wireless and an angelic voice entreated me to *Smoke Chesterfields—The Way To More Smoking Pleasure*!

'F—king Lord Haw-Haw,' I said, with feeling.

I found the room. It was more like a closet. The bed had been made and some cheap undergarments hung to dry from a string tied between the bedpost and the wardrobe. When I looked in the wardrobe I found a copy of my single book, *My Struggle*, in the original Franz Eher first edition, with both volumes bound together in a later binding. Quite a nice little copy, I thought. When I opened to the title page I realised with some surprise that it was inscribed.

Well, well.

It had been a very long time since I last signed a copy of one of those.

So horse-faced Anna Maria was a National Socialist. I barely remembered the woman—most of my attention on visiting Uffing that time was to my wound, and my fetching American-born hostess—but at some point I must have signed a copy for the help.

How the help turned up dead in London was still a mystery, but at least I was getting warmer.

There was no cash lying around, and I was sure Madame Blavatsky had already cleaned up anything of value. They always do, these landladies. They are as greedy as my old friend Goering, and usually just as fat.

Still, I tossed the room. I turned the sheets and looked under the thin mattress. I emptied the wardrobe. Anna Maria wore cheap clothes and even cheaper shoes.

It was when I bent down to look under the bed that I saw a small sheet of paper poking out from underneath the dresser. I cursed, straightened, and tried in vain to shift the heavy lump of wood. At last—with a creak that could have been the wardrobe and could have been my back—it moved. I reached down and stared at the page.

The Saturn Film Company
Cordially Invites You
To a Night You Won't Forget!
Exclusive Screening
Bar Service
Private and Discreet!

MEN ONLY

The Avenue Pavilion Picturehouse, Shaftesbury Avenue

I stared at the flyer.

This was not what I had expected at all.

5

'CINEMA NIGHT IS for members only, sir.'

The usher had the shiny face of an excited teenage boy who'd grown to disappointing manhood. I'd seen faces like that in the trenches, during the war. Hairless rats, we called them. They never made it long out there in Ypres. Of the nearly four thousand men in my regiment, a mere six hundred survived that battle.

'How does one become a member?'

He looked at me dubiously. 'There's a process,' he said. 'A committee and so on.'

'I just want to see the picture.'

He looked from side to side and then stared at me with those big bulging eyes of his. 'You're not with the pigs, are you?'

'Do I look like a policeman?'

'You look like a bum,' he said, and laughed, and it took all my will power not to slap the teeth out of him. 'And it's ten shillings.'

'Ten!' I grabbed him by the shirt and pushed him against the wall. 'You little weasel—'

'This isn't an ordinary picture!' he squeaked.

'I don't have ten shillings.'

I barely had the money for a slice of bread, and my rent was overdue.

'*Five*, if you let me go *now*.'

'You let me in and I don't call the fuzz on you.'

He all but laughed in my face. 'You think they give us trouble? This is a gentlemen's club and gentlemen don't get raided.'

I sighed and let him go.

'All right, then.'

'All right?'

'Sure.'

And I clocked him a coal hammer straight out of the Frank Klaus-Billy Papke fight.

I dragged the unfortunate usher into the cloakroom and left him under a pile of evening coats. Then I sauntered into the cinema proper.

The room was dark and the show had already started. Men sat avidly in the rows. Their eyes were fixed on the screen. They wet their lips. They wriggled uncomfortably in their seats, much like an SS trooper trying to make room for his gun.

I watched the show. The movie was called *Slave-Girls in the Harem*. As a documentary it had little to recommend it. The movement was jerky and it was a silent picture. It was shot in a large room with a large bed by the wall and too many pillows. Four girls stepped into the room and quickly disrobed. They began to perform questionable actions on each other. Then a couple of young men joined them.

I'd seen worse in Vienna in '13 when I was living on the Meldermannstrasse. This had no art. It was mere filth.

I turned my back on the screen. In my younger life I had wanted to be an artist. I was a decent enough painter, I thought. But I had not picked up a brush in years. The men in the audience grunted like the pigs they were. This was no use to me. I sidled past the curtain and made my way up the stairs. The manager's door stood open and a thick cloud of cigar smoke wafted out.

How I loathed the smell!

I came and stood in the doorway. The man behind the desk was fat and had small greedy eyes.

'Hey,' he said, 'you're not supposed to be h—'

He squeaked in alarm and then I was going at him like Hermann Goering with a sponge cake.

'Are you ready to talk?'

He whimpered and spat out blood. It dribbled down his chin. I was kneeling on the floor, looking right into his eyes.

'Do you know Anna Maria Fischer?' I said.

He looked at me blankly.

'Who?'

'German, in her fifties, face like an Ascot winner?'

'No idea, mister.'

'Found dead behind your picture house, by the bins.'

'Oh, her.'

'What was she doing there?' I said.

'No idea, mister.'

I socked him a couple more punches, just as a reminder.

'Look, I don't know nothing! She came round a couple of times asking for work. Or so she claimed. I tried to brush her off but she made a nuisance of herself. Finally... Well, you'd be surprised but there's a market for everything. Some punters really get their kicks watching old ladies get it on, so I finally sent her to the studio.'

'The studio?'

'Saturn Films. They produce all our pictures.'

'And where can I find them?' I said.

He tried to crawl away, then. 'I can't tell you that,' he said. 'I'd get in trouble.'

'You're in trouble now,' I pointed out.

'What you gonna do, beat me up some more?' he said. 'Still better than a .43 in the back of the head.'

I had to acknowledge he had a point.

'Seems we're at an impasse.'

He spat some more blood. 'Seems so.'

I got up. His cigar was still burning in the ashtray and a box of matches sat on the desk. It bore the picture house's advertisement. I shook it and it was half full. I stuck it in my pocket.

'Stay where I can see you,' I said.

'What are you—'

I smiled at him and started opening drawers.

'Hey, you can't *do* tha—'

'Shut the f—k up!' I said. Then, 'Hello... What do we have here?'

'I'm dead,' he said.

'I hope so,' I said. I smiled and waved the invoice at him. It is as I always say. One cannot conduct a criminal enterprise or a genocide without suitable paperwork.

I looked at the address on the invoice, then back at the man.

'*Surbiton?*' I said. 'Where the f—k is Surbiton?'

6

THE SURBITON TRAIN station was a pleasant building done up the year before in an art deco style. I took a moment to appreciate the workmanship. The place itself was some fifteen miles out of London. It was a leafy sort of suburban village, with a greengrocer's and a butcher's on the High Street, several pubs, and a picture house called the Coronation Hall directly opposite the station. It had a high stained glass window of a Star of David, for no reason I could see. It just went to show, Jews were everywhere. Had I my way back in '33 things would have turned out very different. But the communists took control of my beloved Germany, and now Europe groaned under the heel of international Jewry and their Marxist faith.

How I hated Jews! And gypsies, Poles, Slavs, mimes, smokers, and the French. I really hated the French! And

British trains. I hated British trains. I had had to get one from Waterloo to reach Surbiton, though I dodged the fare.

'Excuse me,' I said, to a passer-by. 'Could you direct me to this address, please?'

The man stopped and glared at me. He wore mutton chops and a vest and had the ruddy complexion of a country drunk. He stared at me like I was a piece of dog s—t he found on his foot.

'Not from around here, are you?' he said.

I had nothing to say to that so I didn't.

'Word of advice, my friend. Go back to where you come from. We don't like foreigners here, much, unless you're here to cut the lawns.'

I glared at him in hatred. I used to *be* somebody!

Once upon a time, all of Germany marched to the beat of my drum!

'Up the hill,' he said, relenting. 'Can't miss it.'

'Thank you.'

'Don't mention it.'

With that he stalked off, no doubt to feed his pigs or screw the help—it was that kind of a place.

I walked up St Mark's Hill. Oak trees grew thickly and hid stately Victorian homes. Who knew what kind of depravity they hid. A squirrel ran past me and climbed up a tree. Like Sherlock Holmes before me, I could not look at these scattered houses without the feeling of their isolation and of the impunity with which crime may be committed there.

Surbiton! I thought, savagely. What a f—king s—t-hole!

I found the house. It looked like an old hospital. The gates were closed. There was no sign to suggest occupancy.

It is an old truism of the detective trade—when in doubt, try going through the back.

I went round until I found the entrance. There was a wide low gate for deliveries and I pushed it and went in. Then I jimmied the back door and let myself into the house.

It was the sort of grand old home the British love which is full of cold draughts and no one's cleaned the carpet in years. The sash windows let in the murky grey sunlight. A mouse darted past me and vanished into a hole in the wainscoting.

I tiptoed along the corridor—and came straight to the orgy room.

It was the same room I had seen in the earlier picture. The four poster bed was still there, only now it had two naked men with oiled bodies on it, and they were doing things to each other that would have made even Ernst Röhm blush.

Bright lights were set up around the room and they generated so much heat that everyone was sweating. *Everyone* was the film crew: there were several of them standing all about and there was even a buffet table set against the far wall.

A camera mounted on a dais was pointed at the two

rutting men and a large, imposing man over six feet tall
was barking orders.

'Thrust harder! Thrust harder! That's it! Now turn him
over, Carl! Now gently massage the buttocks!'

I recognised that voice, and the imposing figure, and
the toothbrush moustache like I myself used to sport.
He was as ugly as a mastiff with an erection.

'*Putzi*?' I said.

7

ERNST "PUTZI" HANFSTAENGL turned and looked
at me with utter surprise. It was as though one of his
actors had suddenly sprouted a second schwanz.

'*Adolf*? But... but how?'

'It's Wolf, now,' I told him. 'Just Wolf.'

'But my dear fellow!' He went to embrace me. We
had been close, back in Munich. Back then he had been
a follower, another devotee of National Socialism and
the cause.

Now he was just a pornographer.

'It is so good to *see* you!' he said. 'But what are you
doing here? How on earth did you find me?'

'Anna Maria,' I said, tiredly. The room smelled like a
public bath. One of the actors turned and stared at us
with his schwanz still in his hand.

'Mr Hanfstaengl? I'm losing wood.'

'Take five, boys. There's cold cuts and potato salad on the buffet tables.' He waved them away. The cameraman and the lighting technician and the actors and all the rest of them lit up cigarettes and went off for a bite to eat and a cup of tea. I guess all that hard work made them hungry.

'Anna Maria, Wolf?'

'Anna Maria Fischer. Your old maid.'

He grimaced. 'What about her, Wolf? Come, come, dear fellow. Let's adjourn somewhere we can talk.'

He led me out of the orgy room, down a corridor, and to a cool, dark storage room filled with film canisters. Posters on the walls advertised other Saturn pictures: *Robin's Wood, Gunga Dick, Triumph of the Willies, Follow The Yellow Prick Road,* and *Lust of the Swastika.*

Warning signs said *Do Not Smoke—Highly Flammable Material.*

'Must you bring up this old business?' he said to me then. 'Wolf! Forget this nonsense. Come and work with me! I am making money hand over fist!'

He gestured rudely with his fingers, miming an intimate act.

'She had my name on her person, Putzi,' I said. 'I was visited by the pigs!'

He made a dismissive gesture. 'She always had the hots for you, Wolf. Forget Anna Maria! Since when did you care for the help?'

'Who do you work for, Putzi? You do not have the sort of juice to run this kind of operation by yourself.'

At that he grew sombre. 'There are questions one should not be asking,' he said. 'Not even you.'

I let it go. My silence drew him in.

'She just wasn't no good, Wolf,' he said. A whiny note entered his voice. 'The b—ch was going to rat us out. I had no choice, you see? No choice at all.'

'Tell me.'

He shrugged. 'What is there to tell? She followed me and Helene to London and somehow found out about my little enterprise. Next thing you know she shows up here and starts blackmailing me. What was I to do, Wolf? You've always said it yourself, after all: there are few problems one can't solve with a gun.'

I felt so very tired then. 'How is Helene?' I said.

'Good, good,' he said, distractedly. 'Misses the Fatherland, though, as do I. It is terrible, what happened, Wolf. Terrible.'

He looked less than upset at the humiliating defeat of National Socialism. Just imagine had I won! I would have changed the *world*!

I took out the box of matches that I liberated at the picture house from my pocket. I shook it and it made a little rattling noise.

'Oh, there's no smoking in here, Wolf. On account of the film stock. It's the nitrates, you see.'

'I don't smoke.'

A confused look came into his eyes. 'That's what I thought,' he said. 'Then what—'

I smiled at him almost kindly as I struck the match

and held it. The flame was very bright. A look of horror came into his eyes then and he said, 'You wouldn't—'

I began to whistle the Horst Wessel Song. Putzi barrelled past me in his haste to escape. I turned and tossed the match and, still whistling, left the room.

Behind me, without much fuss, the film stock caught fire.

8

I STOOD UNDER a rather lovely oak tree that must have been standing there a hundred years or more, and watched the studio burn. It burned with all the dedication of a race theory scholar reading Hans Günther's *Short Ethnology of the German People* for the first time. I mean, intensely.

I did not believe in justice, which is for the weak.

But I believed in order—order above all things.

I believed in the manifest destiny of the Aryan race, in Kaiserschmarrn and apple strudel, and that dogs were better than cats. I was definitely a dog person. I believed in vegetarianism, and that smoking was a filthy habit and that the only thing worse than a Pole was a Jew. I believed *I* should have won in 1933, and that the swastika flag should have hung over the Reichstag building—but it wasn't.

I believed in Geli Raubal until she killed herself to

spite me. I believed I should have been paid a higher advance than the measly £300 my British publishers, Hurst and Blackett, paid me for *My Struggle*. And I believed the *f—king* trains should *f—king* run on *time*!

I believed in doing the right thing—whatever the cost.

I stood and watched the firemen arrive and the hoses go, and the black smoke rising. Then I crumpled the postcard from Uffing and let it drop to the ground, and I made my way back down the hill.

* * *

IN ANOTHER TIME and place there's Shomer, walking back. The night is cold and there is no firewood with which to light a fire.

Meeting his friend Yenkl by the Yiddish Theatre, Shomer shows him the postcard from America. After a moment, his friend chuckles without mirth.

'There is a story told of the writer, Ödön von Horváth,' he says. 'He was walking in the Bavarian Alps once when he discovered the skeleton of a hiker with his rucksack still intact. Von Horváth opened the bag and found a postcard that said "Having a wonderful time".'

Shomer nods, for all that he is distracted. He thinks of Fanya and the children, and of what the next winter will bring. If there is another winter.

If it is not, already, too late.

'*What did he do with it?*' he says.
'*What?*'
'*With the postcard.*'
Yenkl nods, sagely, and shrugs.
'*He posted it,*' he says.

FIVE

THE SPEAR OF DESTINY

From beyond the ghetto walls come the peal of church bells; pure and clear, clear and pure the sound fills the night above the ghetto, and Shomer and the children stop and listen to it, spellbound in their captivity.

Beyond the walls, ordinary citizens are on their way to church and then to All Hallows' feast and celebration. But inside, day turns to night like every other cycle of the world as it spins on its axis. the soldiers with their guns watch over the walls and the Jews inside crowded like so many birds for the slaughter. Only they do not fatten them, here, they starve them, the more efficiently to dispose of later. And Shomer's daughter shivers in her thin coat, and he lifts her in his arms, how hard he cradles her as though it is in this way that he could pass to her some warmth, to stave away the onslaught of winter. And Bina listens to the church bells and she smiles, and it breaks Shomer's heart that she does. And Avrom says, Papa, Papa, when can we go home again?

And Shomer says nothing.

They walk on to the Yiddish theatre, held in the hall of the old gymnasium. Shomer pays the price of admission and ushers his children in with the rest. They sit, shivering, on their coats. How much he loves them, he thinks, Avrom, Bina—his children. He remembers each birth, how he paced outside before being allowed in, at last, and how he held each of them in his arms, upon this miraculous entry into the world, and he their father, sworn to love and protect them.

And he thinks, how long do we have, how many days how many hours? For in the ghetto they speak, in hushed tones, of the trains headed east. Resettlement, some say. And others shake their heads and mutter, No, no.

But now his old friend Yenkl comes on stage draped in a cape, with oversized teeth protruding comically. And the children clap, excited, for tonight on this night of the goyishe day of All Saints, the theatre's staging a picture. Shomer had seen it once, when there were still cinemas, and he remembers how much he loved it, and he wishes he could escape into the screen of the past, and pull his children after him for safety. The lights dim. I bid you welcome, Yenkl says. And Shomer blinks back no, not tears, he has none left of those to shed, but something. And he retreats into the only safety he has left, his writer's mind, nothing but useless fantasy. And he thinks, no, it is only fantasy which is left to us, the dying, for comfort in our final days.

A cheap tale and only that, an entertainment. We have that, still, as yet.

1

HIS NAME WAS Heinrich Himmler and he was what the English, in their barbaric pig sty tongue, call a c—t.

How I hated the English! I hated the smell of boiled beef and soiled terrycloth nappies and Gentlemen's Choice Old Spice, their noisy overcrowded streets ill-lit with gas lamps, I hated the ludicrous grooming of their facial hair, like old Prussian officers, and their women, who looked like old Prussian officers themselves. Back in Germany I had been a leader of men! For a decade we waged dirty street war against the communists, but then, in the elections of 1933, I was inexplicably defeated.

Hitler! Hitler! How they chanted my name! Then the bastard Jew commies threw me in a concentration camp and it was there that I lost several teeth and nearly lost my leg, which still aches in cold weather—which on this godforsaken island means, constantly. How I escaped that camp, and into England, is another matter. Now I went by my old *nom de guerre* of Wolf.

Just Wolf.

'Wolf, Wolf, Wolf, *Wolf!*' the c—t Himmler said. I stared at him in hatred. I had not seen him since the Fall in '33. Then, he had been the head of my militia, the *Schutzstaffel*, or SS. There had been 52,000 of them, men ready to serve my cause. Then, the Fall. Now that fat fuck Ernst Thälmann of the KPD was *Reichskanzler*, and I was an out of work private eye in London, living above a Jew baker's shop and paying rent I could ill afford, in this Year of Our Lord, 1938.

'What do you want, Heinrich? I thought you were dead.'

He smirked. 'You mean you wished I was?'

'I'd hoped someone would have helped you commit suicide with a round of bullets in the back, if that's what you mean,' I said.

'Those men you sent after me soon went to feed the fish in the Havel, and you should have been dancing the Spandau Ballet a long time ago, old friend. Yet here we are.'

He looked good, the bastard. His face had a sheen of health and his suit must have cost nearly as much as a Rothschild's *kipah*.

'You escaped?'

'I *decamped*. I spent some time in Transylvania, then France…' He patted his stomach. 'You know me,' he said. 'I can't complain.'

I felt awfully tired. He'd hunted me down to a tea shack in Soho where I'd sat in the back, drinking some awful concoction and watching the door. I always watched doors. Nothing good ever came through them.

'What do you *want*, Heinrich? I won't ask you again.'

'I was told you are the man to speak to. If one needs to locate missing things.'

'What did you lose? Besides your honour and my respect.'

'Wolf, please. There is no need for *banter*.'

I wanted to strangle him, but the English constabulary get heated up over publicly committed murders. I could never understand it. Back when I was running things, my men killed on the streets of Munich and Berlin with impunity. Different strokes and all that...

'You want *me* to work for *you?*' I said.

'Is that so hard?' he said. He took out his wallet and extracted a thick wad of notes. I stared at the money.

'It's kosher, Wolf,' he said, and laughed at his own little joke.

'What are you looking for?' I said.

He sat down across from me, and he was no longer smiling. His eyes shone with the devotion of the true fanatic. A terrible feeling came upon me then, for I had known Himmler and his weird obsessions, and every sense I had was tingling with the thought that I should either shoot him or run.

'The Spear of Destiny, Wolf!' he said. 'It's in London! At least, it will be soon, if it isn't here already. The real one, I mean. Not that scheisse fake they have in the Hofburg in Vienna.'

I buried my head in my hands. My morning s—t that morning had been drier than an English whore's muffin, I hadn't had a client in three weeks and my rent was overdue, and it had rained all f—king day, in that sort of thin drizzle that has the consistency and smell of British beer... but you know me, I can't complain.

All I needed now was Heinrich f—king Himmler and his occult obsessions. The holy lance! I saw it in the

Hofsburg back in '12. Then, as an impressionable youth of 23, it had felt to me as though I had held it before, as though I myself was some mythical reincarnation of the legendary leaders of history—Charlemagne! Barbarossa! Sigismund! I imagined myself holding it in my hands and leading the forces of Germany in total war against the world—conquering first the ancestral Sudetenland, then the rest of Czechoslovakia, before annexing Austria back into the Greater German Reich and invading Poland.

After that—the world!

Or so I thought, back then. Now, there was only one question on my mind—

'This spear,' I said. 'Expensive, is it?'

'But Wolf, it is *priceless!*' Himmler said. 'One could hardly put a price to the spear which pierced the Saviour's side!'

'I thought you gave up on Catholicism.'

He nodded thoughtfully. 'Yes,' he said. 'But the spear is an object of great antiquity—and great power, Wolf. A man who possesses it could never be defeated on the field of battle.'

'And if you put a leaf of mint in your shoe it will keep it smelling fresh all day,' I said. Lord! Spare me from my former Nazi comrades and their eternal obsession with the occult!

'I can pay you. Handsomely!'

He sounded desperate, now. I stared at the money. The very thought of working for a former underling—

for this loathsome toad—this enormous c—t—the very *thought* was repugnant to me.

'I would need the fee upfront,' I said.

'Of course,' he said, smoothly. He peeled off several notes and handed them to me. 'And when you find it for me, Wolf, then you could simply name your price.'

'You want it that much?'

'I must have it. I have been searching for it for a very long time.'

'All right,' I said, tiredly. 'Then tell me where to start.'

2

THE SPEAR OF Destiny, or the Holy Lance, is one of those relics that used to be traded with great enthusiasm back in the Middle Ages, and which clearly had its avid collectors even unto the modern day. It was the spear that, according to the Gospel of John, pierced Jesus' side as he hung on the cross. Like all such relics of dubious authenticity, there are several claims as to the "true" lance. There is one in Rome, and another in Vienna, and yet another one in some s—t hole in Armenia, or whatever they're calling the place nowadays. In that, it joins similar objects such as the Turin Shroud, the Crown of Thorns, the True Cross and the Veil of Veronica—not to mention the Holy Grail, of course.

Back in the Middle Ages, one could easily purchase

a piece of the cross, or a fragment of bone from Jesus' body, or any number of other ridiculous fakes manufactured for easy profiteering from the delusions of the weak. I myself had abandoned my early Catholicism but, unlike Himmler, I was not much given to the occult nonsense that his ilk chased like so many moonbeams in a meadow.

The man was a dangerous buffoon, but a buffoon who had grown fat and wealthy in the years that followed the Fall. Like many who were attracted to my National Socialist movement in the early days, he was a ruthless and practical man who merely saw an opportunity to enrich himself on the back of my ideology. He may have bet on the wrong winner that time, but he soon enough fell back on his feet. This is the thing about rats: they are so very hard to get rid of. And there was hardly a rat as big and as diseased as Heinrich Himmler.

God, how I wished he was still running my beloved SS!

As a leader, I had use for such rats. These days, all I could do was take their money.

* * *

'*I AM… DRACULA*,' Bela Lugosi said. I sat in the dark watching the flickering light of the projector as Renfield turned and stared at the count on the screen.

'*I bid you welcome.*'

I was at the Pavilion on Shaftesbury Avenue, not far

from my office. They'd cleaned up their act a little since I busted their pornographic operation a few months earlier. But I wasn't there to watch Lugosi being an ass on screen. I was trailing a man who had his own interest in the Spear of Destiny.

Himmler had hunted for it in Transylvania. From there he had tracked its whereabouts to France and the Carmargue, and to an old Gypsy church, but was too late to acquire it. Now he had it on good authority that the spear was on its way to London by sea, if it wasn't there already.

I believed none of it, of course. Or rather, I believed that *he* believed it, for I had seen the sort of things Heinrich Himmler believed in, and even on a good day the man was as weak in the head as a soft boiled egg. What *hadn't* he believed in! Veganism and nudism and Satanism and occultism and... well, Nazism, of course, but I rather flattered myself that *that* particular ideology wasn't *entirely* insane... whatever my numerous detractors claimed.

The man I was trailing was named Pound. He was a miserable looking f—k in his fifties and a poet who made his living sucking my old friend Mussolini's c—k, and twice on Sundays. I never had much time for the Italians, myself. Benito had been a useful fool for a time, but the man could hardly keep his d—k in his pants and he had the intellectual capacity of a wilted asparagus.

It was not hard to find this Pound. He was staying in a dingy hotel in Bloomsbury, and I understood from

Himmler that, like himself, Pound was also after the spear.

'I last had a run-in with the man in Pisa,' Himmler said, darkly. 'He was quite an admirer of yours, as it turns out, back in the day. We had a good chat—well, I mean, my men gave him a good beating while I conversed over a glass of port—mostly about how the next time I run into him I'll kill him. But I can't, Wolf! Mussolini considers him useful.'

'Mussolini!' I said. 'The man's a buffoon!'

'Yet a fashionable one.'

I trailed Pound across London, as he met with various literary figures of little interest to me—Eliot, the degenerate American poet, was the only one I recognised—and he seemed to do little else but that— that and drinking, I mean. He was dressed in trousers made of green billiard cloth, a pink coat, a blue shirt, a hand-painted tie and a single, large blue earring. He looked like an ageing French prostitute. By the time we'd reached the Pavilion the man was swaying on his feet and swearing loudly, going on about Chinese poetry, the tenets of Italian Futurism, and his undying hatred of the Jews. I half-expected him to break into the Horst Wessel Song at any moment. Instead, he swayed his way to the cinema, where I saw, with a sinking heart, that a Blackshirts demonstration was taking place. These minions of Oswald Mosley were the cut-rate copy of my own superior SS—grocers' boys and clerks' brats and the illegitimate sons of inbred aristocrats with the table manners of pigs and with wives to match. They were dressed in Mosley's own Futurist uniforms of black parachutist garments, held at the waist with a black belt and a shiny metal buckle, and with a single lightning bolt on the breast. They looked like an expedition to an alien planet that they intended to, sooner or later, pillage and rape.

Pound went cheerily through them, shaking hands, slapping backs and generally being a grand dame for the cause. When I approached, however, the sons-of-whores turned on me and viewed me with suspicion, blocking my way.

'Excuse me,' I said. 'I shall be late for the picture!'

'Not from around here, are you?'

'What's it to you, sonny?'

'This is English land, for English people. Go back to where you came from, you f—king kraut!'

'Yes,' chimed in another. 'We don't want stinking foreigners coming over here, do we, lads?'

'No, we don't!'

'Get back to where you came from!'

'Stink of cabbage and s—t.'

'It's called *sauerkraut* and it's very healthy!' I shouted. 'You little f—king c—k-sucking *s—ts*, do you not know who I *am!*'

'No idea, mate.'

'You all look the same to me.'

'I could have ruled the *world!*'

'You don't look like you could rule *d—k,*' someone said, which I thought was rather rude, and also sounded strangely American. Then they were on me, shoving and punching until I went down, and then they *really* got to work. As the group of young men began to viciously kick me, I could do nothing but curl into a ball and try to protect my head and private parts. Their steel-capped boots found the soft spots in my body and would have broken my bones had not some old biddy, no doubt drunk on cheap sherry and perhaps with fond memories of the Great War in her addled brain, began to hit the Blackshirts with her handbag while screaming curses at them, until they sheepishly broke away from breaking my bones and, if not dispersed, at least left me be.

I stood up, wincing with pain, and hobbled into the cinema. I washed the blood off my face in the restroom, procured a ticket, and made my way into the darkened theatre. I saw Pound and sat a few rows behind him.

The film began.

'*I have chartered a ship to take us to England. We will be leaving... tomorrow... evening.*'

It was then that I saw her.

She was nearing sixty then, and I daresay she wasn't much of a beauty in her youth, either. She had the face of a Jewish laundress. A weak mouth and mean eyes and she wore a black mink fur coat, as though draping herself with a poor dead animal's skin could make her seem more glamorous. I recognised her, of course. Her name was Margherita Sarfatti and she was Il Duce's ideologue and whore.

She wend her way to Pound and sat in the row behind him. They spoke in low voices, but I could hear them all the same.

'Do you have it yet?'

'My source says it arrives tomorrow on board the *Hestia*, from Reykjavik.'

'Reykjavik? What in the—'

His voice was barely perceptible to me. '*He* is after it, now.'

'*Cohn?* Cohn is *here?*'

'*The captain dead, tied to the wheel. Horrible tragedy! Horrible tragedy.*'

'He must not be allowed to gain access to the spear!'

'We must have it for Italy, Pound. For Il Duce!'

'*Why, he's mad! Look at his eyes! Why, the man's gone crazy!*'

'Don't you think I *know* that, you Jewish harpy?'

'You'd better watch the way you speak, Pound. Or you won't be the first foreign poet to suffer a fatal accident in Italy.'

'What does he *see* in you?' the man said, with surprising bitterness.

'What does he see in *you!*' she said.

'I am a great poet!'

'And I am a great—'

'Lay? I doubt it, Margherita.'

'...*strategist*, you degenerate American *fanculo*.'

'F—k *you*, Margherita, you dried up *b—ch*—'

Heads were turning, and I'd heard enough. I got up from my seat and left the cinema, Dracula's voice echoing behind me in the darkened auditorium.

'*There are far worse things... awaiting man... than death.*'

'Oh, shut *up*, Bela!' I said.

Exit Wolf, Stage Left.

3

I WALKED AWAY along Shaftesbury Avenue. *Idiot's Delight* was showing at the Apollo. Children went guising along the road dressed as tiny little skeletons, and by the Palace Theatre on Cambridge Circus a merry bonfire was burning, and as I came closer I saw that the people around it were feeding it books.

'Stop!' I said. 'What are you doing!'

But the people ignored me. They seemed hypnotised by the fire. I loved books! The right books, of course, not books by Jews or anything degenerate, but Schiller! Goethe! Karl May! Back in Germany I had thousands of books in my library, many of them personal gifts to me from their authors. I myself was an author! Admittedly, *My Struggle* had not done as well as I'd initially hoped, but it *should* have been a best-seller! It is a truth universally acknowledged that an author in possession of a good manuscript is soon in want of a publisher... how I had been betrayed! I, who could have led Germany to victory!

'f—k off, kraut,' someone said. Had I been speaking aloud?

'Yeah, piss off back to your own f—king country!' an old woman said, and pushed me. I was so startled that I fell over. As I lay there I saw the books they were throwing in the fire. It was all manner of garbage from the book stalls on the Charing Cross Road—nothing but an assortment with no sense or sensibility—'No!' I said, in pain. 'Not Agatha Christie!'

I was very fond of her books.

But it was no use. These barbarians—these *animals!*—they just kept throwing these books into the bonfire, that All Hallows' Eve, with not a care in the world as to their ideological purity or otherwise. I think... I think they just liked the feel of the burning.

And so, not wishing to be attacked again, I pulled myself up and continued on my way.

I hopped a bus outside Patterson's Pills, headed east. I sat on the upper deck and watched the city go past beyond the window. We went along the river until the docks came into view. I climbed down and walked. The Thames was wider here, and ships were resting at the quays. Even at this hour there was movement along the pathways. I searched among the ships but could not see the *Hestia.* I approached the shipping office, where a taciturn man around my age was the only one about.

He was reading a book called *The Way Out* that looked cheaply produced.

'Help you?' he said, laying down the book at my approach. Strangely, he had an American accent.

'Looking for information on a ship, the *Hestia*,' I said. 'Out of Reykjavik.'

'The *Hestia*...' he said, and looked at me sharply. 'Why do you ask? It carries fish from the Norwegian Sea, and you don't strike me as a man in the fish business.'

'What do men in the fish business look like?' I said.

'They look less fishy,' he said, and sneered at me.

'Listen to me,' I said, 'you imbecile. There is precious cargo on that ship and I must have it. You strike me as a man without recourse to vast funds.'

'That is true,' he allowed. 'I am an author, you see. Name of Keeler.'

'Well, I never f—king heard of you,' I said. 'But I imagine the pay's poor.'

'It is. I am on a visit to London to research a novel, and I took on this job. Do you have an offer for me?'

'I could pay you handsomely. My client is wealthy.'

'Your client?'

'I am a private detective,' I said. 'Name's Wolf.'

'I see. And the cargo in question?'

'It is some sort of an archaeological find. A Roman spear.'

'You intrigue me, Mr Wolf.'

'Here,' I said. I handed him a wad of cash. Himmler had been generous.

Keeler took it without changing expression. 'And if I can get hold of it?' he said.

'Then bring it to me.' I wrote down the address for him. 'I could triple the money.'

'Triple it, eh? Very well. But I make no promises.'

I nodded.

'*Auf wiedersehen*, Mr Keeler.'

'Yeah, right, see you.'

'I sincerely hope so.'

With that, I left him. I knew he would to it. You knew where you were with writers. They were always impoverished, and they had no morals. They were as selfish as cats and as ruthless as cuckoo birds. I felt quite satisfied with myself as I walked away and back into town. I was somewhere near London Bridge when I heard footsteps behind me, and the purr of a car, but I thought nothing of it at first. Then I felt one pair of arms and then another on either side of me, as two large and rather intimidating men in dark and expensive-looking suits grabbed me and hustled me forward.

'Wait,' I said, 'wait, wait, hold on, we can talk about this—'

A black Mercedes limousine pulled to the curb and the doors opened. The two men bundled me inside without ceremony and shut the doors.

I was trapped.

4

THE CAR TOOK off with a soft purr of the engine. For just a moment, it felt good to be sitting inside a miracle of German engineering again.

Then I saw the man sitting opposite me. He had a shiny forehead and the eyes of a gold trader and a face meaner than my father's after he'd had a few drinks. My father would hit me with his belt but I never cried, I refused to cry, a good Aryan boy does not cry. I did not cry at his funeral.

This man was not my father but he had that same mean look in his eyes. He lifted his hand and smacked me across the face, and his ring dug into my flesh and ripped through it. I winced in hatred and pain.

'So you're the gumshoe,' he said.

He too had an American accent.

'May I know who is addressing me?' I said, masking my hatred with politeness. 'I'm afraid I have not had the pleasure.'

'What pleasure, you little c—k sucker?' he said. His two men crowded me on either side. I would have ripped his eyes out but for them—and for the dainty little gun that materialised in his hand. He pointed it at me.

'I want it,' he said. 'The spear. Where is it?'

'I don't know.'

'Listen, *bucher*, I asked you a question. And when Harry Cohn asks a question, he doesn't ask it twice.'

'So you're Cohn. The movie producer. Your films are s—t.'

'I made *Lost Horizons*, you f—king *dummkopf*.'

'I saw *Mussolini Speaks*. The first five minutes, anyway, before I wanted to shoot myself.'

'I could do it for you,' he said, smiling widely and waving the gun menacingly. 'Just say the word, kraut.'

'Look, Cohn, I don't know where it is.'

'But you're looking for it? That s—t Himmler hired you, didn't he?'

'What if he had?'

'How does a nobody like you know Heinrich Himmler, anyway?' he said. Then he stared at me closely. 'You know, you almost look like…' Then he began to laugh.

'I just have that kind of face,' I said.

'You won't have much of a face left if you don't answer my questions.'

'I told you, I don't know where it is! What do you want it for, anyway?'

'A *major* motion picture, gumshoe. It will be about this archaeologist who searches for the Spear of Destiny and fights the communists for it. At the end of the movie he uses the spear to vanquish his enemies—swish! Swash! Big fireworks display, the works—I've got the guy who did *Metropolis* on contract.'

'*Metropolis* was degenerate art.'

'You're a f—king degenerate.'

'That's all it is to you? A *prop*?'

'That, and I get to stick it to the others. *They* want it,

so isn't that enough reason to take it from them? I like taking things from people.'

'I can see that.'

'So?'

The gun was in my face and his men were on either side of me and it looked like I'd have to change my tune or pay the piper, as the fellow said.

'Look,' I said. 'Let's be reasonable.'

'Oh?'

'I told you I don't have it, but I might be able to find it for you.'

'Is that so?'

'Himmler is an ass,' I said. 'And I bet you can pay better.'

'I could buy Buckingham Palace and f—k the old queen if I want to,' he said. I let that go past, for all that it was an utterly disgraceful way to speak about the monarchy. If only it was I holding the gun!

But I wasn't. And so, 'If I can get it,' I said. 'Is that worth a reward?'

'You could name your price,' he said.

'Then let me work for you. I can bring it to you, Cohn! F—k those others. Just set me free.'

'You really *are* a rat, aren't you,' he said. But he made the gun disappear, and he relaxed back in his seat.

'Drink?' he said.

'Sure.'

'Boychiks?'

The man on my left reached for a cabinet that opened

at the press of a button, revealing an array of bottles and glasses inside. He poured a scotch for Cohn and something complicated and colourful for me.

'What is it?' I said, sniffing in suspicion.

'A Mickey Finn,' Cohn said, and sniggered.

'I am not familiar with that,' I said, stiffly. 'And I never touch alcohol.'

'Just drink it, you piece of s—t, before I change my mind,' he said.

I took a gulp and grimaced. It hit me worse than an uppercut from Jack Dempsey.

'Where can I find you?' I said.

'I shall be staying at the Ritz.'

'Good. Good.' I began to giggle. He looked at me with amusement.

'What's so funny?'

'You Jews,' I said. 'You're such c—'

My mouth was moving but no words came out. My lips felt like alien, rubbery appendages. The world went in and out of focus and the last thing I saw was Cohn's smile, and then the world went dark and, for a while, everything stopped.

5

I WOKE UP to the smell of garbage. My head ached indomitably. I was lying by the bins outside Kettner's and flies were buzzing over the stench of congealed *Bourguignonne*. I dry-retched, for I had not eaten anything in hours, and dragged myself upright. That c—k sucker Cohn must have drugged me. It was no longer night, and a wan sun shone down on the dirty streets. London is ugliest in daytime. Night suits it better, and in winter the fog lies low and acts to further obscure the hideous old streets, and the repulsive characters who wandered them. I made my way back to my office on Berwick Street. The bakery was open and the smell enticing. I stepped inside, where my landlord, Edelmann, was serving behind the counter.

'Herr Edelmann,' I said, stiffly.

'Mr Wolf?' he looked at me in concern. 'Is everything all right?'

'What's it to you?'

'It's just, you look a little…'

'I'm *fine*,' I said. 'And I would like two *Berliner pfannkuchen* and an *apfelstrudel*.'

The truth is I have always had a sweet tooth.

He wrapped the pastries and handed them to me without further comment. I peeled a note and handed it to him.

'And the rent, Mr Wolf? I would not ask, only that it is due, you see.'

'I will get you your d—n money, Edelmann.'

'I don't doubt it, Mr Wolf. Nevertheless, it is due, you see.'

'Here!' I said, and shoved the rest of the money at him. He took it from me with a sorrowful expression.

'Till next time, then, Mr Wolf.'

'Till next time, Edelmann.'

'Enjoy your pfannkuchen!'

'F—k off,' I muttered, but under my breath, as I left his shop. My pocket was lighter but my rent was paid, and my mouth was full of vanilla cream. Things could be worse! I thought almost cheerfully, as I climbed the stairs up to my office above the shop. I pushed open the door, which was when I saw the corpse.

6

KEELER LAY CURLED on the floor in a pool of blood. A spear stuck out of his side. It was a very old spear. I pulled it out of the wound. Keeler had been killed with the Spear of Destiny, and someone had thoughtfully left it for me to find.

I had to get rid of the corpse.

It was clear someone was out to frame me. I didn't know how far behind the police were, but I was certain they will soon make an appearance. Those f—king pigs! Who could it be? Who could have done this to me? To *me!*

'Wolfy? Is that you?'

'Martha, how many times do I have to tell you to stay out of my f—king office!'

'Oh, dear,' she said, pushing the door open and leer-ing at me through the cake of makeup on her face. 'I hope this isn't another one of your clients.'

The seeds the old whore sold to tourists in Trafalgar Square to feed the pigeons were posion. So was she.

'Listen, you have to help me.'

'Anything for you, Wolfy, you dear, *dear* man!' she said. 'Do you have money?'

'Get out!'

I pushed her out and followed, shutting the door behind me. 'Quick, let's go in your room.'

'It's a bit early for me to go the full gallop,' she said, 'but I can give you a canter, Wolf, if you give me a hand.' And she laughed uproariously.

'Shut *up*, Martha, you disease-riddled whore!'

Her hand rose and she smacked me across the face hard enough that I could feel it in my teeth. She looked at me and leered. 'You *like* that, don't you, Nancy-boy?'

'Shut up.' My voice was hoarse.

'I could do it for you, Wolf. For a price. I could hit you all you want…'

'Shut up! Please…'

Her hand was on my gaying instrument, squeezing painfully.

'Stop…'

She released me abruptly and leered again, her hideous old face as monstrous as a heathen idol's.

'I'm *retired*, Wolfy. You *know* that.'

'Listen, Martha!' I pushed her into her bedsit, across the hall from mine, and shut the door. I still held the blood-stained spear. 'Forget all that. You have to hide this for me.'

'For free?'

'No, damn it. Here.' I shoved some money at her. My bankroll was quickly vanishing, I realised ruefully. 'Now shut the door and keep quiet while I go get rid of the body.'

'If I had a penny for every time a man said that to me…' she said dreamily.

I shook my head in despair, left her in her bedsit and returned to my office.

The door was open.

The corpse was gone.

7

'SON OF A *b—ch*!'

'What's the matter, Wolfy?'

'That f—king guy, he wasn't *dead* dead!'

'If I had a penny for every time a man said that to me…'

'Oh shut u—' I gave up.

I stared at the floor. Bloody footprints led to the door and down the stairs, and a note had been left for me, '*The Spear of Destiny brings only sorrow*'. Next to it, that hack Keeler had drawn a skull. Why, I had no idea. Maybe the guy just liked skulls.

'Anyway, it doesn't matter,' I said. 'Without a corpse no one can accuse me of murder, can they?'

'I suppose not.'

'And I *do* have the spear. That's a stroke of luck and no mistake.'

'It looks like a piece of old junk, Wolfy.'

'Takes one to know one?'

'Really!' she said, huffily.

I ignored Martha. I paced my office, back and forth, back and forth. Things were going my way for once! The question was, how could I make the most out of the situation? The way I saw it, I had a valuable—rare—priceless!—object in my *exclusive* possession. Sure, Himmler offered me cash. But so had Cohn. And as for that shit poet, Pound, and that Italian woman he was apparently in cahoots with—well, they looked as starved as dormice but they had Mussolini's ear, didn't they? And, presumably, a hand in the old lecher's pocket. This was the problem with Italians—they were led by their dicks, and sooner or later the biggest dick was in charge.

No, I had to *maximise* my earning potential. With that in mind, I began to hum a cheerful tune, and I sat down at my desk, put my feet up (ignoring the blood on the soles) and wrote three notes, which I sealed each into three neat, white envelopes. It made me think, rather fondly, of Agatha Christie, and that funny little Belgian detective of hers. I had always rather fancied the idea of invading Belgium. It was a little s—t hole of a country where they didn't even know if they were Dutch or French. I would have made them Germany's slaves, and grateful for it.

I began to laugh. And laugh, and laugh, until I couldn't stop and tears came.

Then I left my office and went to deliver the letters.

* * *

IN THE DARK hall of the Yiddish theatre in the old gymnasium, Shomer blinks back tears as the lights rise over the stage. The actors take a bow. There is Yenkl, resplendent in his black Count's robes. There the graveyard, with the fake fog lying low over the tombstones. And Shomer shivers in the cold, a hint of premonition, and he gathers the children to him as though, by holding them like this, so close, he could not only keep them warm but keep them safe, forever. There they rise, the audience, shuffling and stretching, wrapped in poor coats, in ill-fitted shoes, and their bellies empty and their eyes hollow. But it is not yet time, there is yet hope, there is, yet, a life, however meagre. And he hugs Avrom and Bina to him and holds them against the encroaching night.

8

'YOU MUST BE wondering why I gathered you all here,' I said.

'Listen, you dolt,' Cohn said. 'I know why I'm here. Why are *they* here?'

They were an ungainly assembly. Cohn to one side, Himmler with a scowl to another, and Pound and the Sarfatti woman with their backs to the ancient walls. We were down underneath St. Martin-in-the-Fields, in the old crypt. I needed somewhere quiet and private to conduct this business.

'You all want the spear,' I said. 'The question is, who of you can afford it?'

'You little untrustworthy bastard,' Cohn said. 'You know what an honest man is, Wolf? A man who, when he's bought, *stays* bought.'

I ignored him, as did the others. Himmler licked his lips. 'Do you have it, Wolf?'

'Here,' I said. I brought out the spear. It was wrapped carefully in grey paper. The others stared at the bundle in my hands.

'I will give you two thousand pounds,' Margherita Sarfatti said.

'Three thousand,' Himmler said.

'Four,' Cohn said. 'You c—k sucker.'

Sarfatti consulted with Pound in a low voice. 'Five,' she announced.

'Six!' Cohn said.

'You bastard, Wolf, I thought we were *friends*,' Himmler said. 'Seven thousand pounds. With this spear, I shall be the one to become the new Führer of Germany!'

'You are not fit to lick my shoes,' I told him. The truth was, when I had held the spear, I felt nothing.

The lights in the crypt were dim. Boxes were lying every which way. The church used it for storage, and I had broken in.

'*Ten* thousand pounds,' Cohn said. 'But let us see it, Wolf. Let us see the Spear of Destiny!'

I shrugged. The others exchanged glances. Could they beat Cohn for the price?

I unwrapped the paper. The spear felt light in my hand. I imagined that Roman centurion, Longinus, as he must have held it two thousand years earlier, standing before the man hung on the cross. I myself would have changed the world, like Jesus. If only I hadn't been betrayed!

'Here it is!' I shouted. I held it high, shaking it at them. 'The Holy Lance which pierced the Saviour's side! The weapon held by Charlemagne when he united Europe! I can feel it now, its power calls to me, I who would have succeeded Sigismund!'

Spittle flew from my lips. I would be d—ned if I gave it to them, I thought! For too long I had been trodden upon and ignored—now, at last, I could claim back my destiny, return to Germany, resume my rightful place, declare a war upon the world!

'Mine! *Mine*!' I screamed.

'F—k this,' Cohn said, and he pulled out a gun. In seconds, guns appeared in the hands of Himmler, Pound and the Italian woman. They didn't seem to know who to aim at—me, or each other.

'Give me the spear, Wolf.'

'Never!'

'Toss it! Toss it now!'

'N—'

A shot nicked my arm. The f—king Jewish woman *shot* me!

I dropped the spear and it clattered to the centre, between us. I held my arm and cursed. None of them moved. Their guns were trained on each other.

'Nobody move.'

'I will take it, for Il Duce.'

'I will take it, for Germany!'

'I will take it to shove up your asses,' Cohn said.

'Is this *it*?' Pound said.

'What?'

'It's just…'

'What!'

'It's just that it doesn't look *Roman*,' Pound said. 'It's too short, and the shape of the head is wrong.'

'What?' Himmler dropped his gun and bent down to look at the spear, oblivious to the threat from the others. He raised his head and glared at me in fury.

'It's nothing but a cheap fake!'

'What?' I said. 'Wait, you've got the wrong end of the stick, old friend, that's not—'

I waved my hands desperately and the four of them turned on me. 'No, no, no, you don't underst—'

'Son of a *b—ch!*'

Then they were on me, the bastards. Guns forgotten, they were possessed in the fury of spiteful children, hitting me with fists and nails until I fell to the cold floor of the crypt, and then they were on me with abandon, kicking and screaming and calling me every name under the sun, until the pain became unbearable and their voices became the drone of waves against a distant shore, and I drowned.

9

WHEN I CAME to, they were gone, and so was the spear. I lay on the floor of the crypt, crying in pain, until I saw a shuddering beam of light, followed by footsteps, and someone cried out, 'S—t!'

It was the night watchman for the church. He pointed the light at me but made no attempt to help me up. 'Sleeping rough, old boy?' he said. 'You'll have to move it, I'm afraid. Breaking in is a crime, you know.'

'I am not...' I said, tears of humiliation and rage choking my voice.

'There, there. Toddle off now, there's a good lad.'

'I am not...!'

I gave up. Somehow, I pulled myself upright. When I reached for my wallet, I found that it, too, was gone. One of the bastards had *robbed* me!

I dragged myself home along the dark streets. The last of the guisers went past me, ghostly figures holding lanterns, tiny skeleton children and monstrous ogres. On Berwick Street the bakery was closed. I climbed upstairs to my room and collapsed on the bed. This was my struggle.

A knock on the door, and that fat cow Martha came in, holding a half-full bottle of cheap schnapps. She saw the state I was in and clucked.

'Make some room, Wolfy,' she said. She pushed me with her arse and sat herself comfortably on the narrow bed beside me, her back to the wall. She took a meditative sip of schnapps.

'Things didn't go well?'

'No, Martha. They have not been going well for some time.'

'Schnapps?'

'I never drink... schnapps.'

She burped. I closed my eyes. The stench was disgusting. Outside the window, the first rays of light could be seen.

'Happy Halloween, Wolf,' she said.

* * *

WALKING BACK WITH the children Shomer hears, beyond the ghetto walls, the peal of church bells. Beyond the walls children run, laughing and playing, their bellies full. Beyond the walls life goes on as though nothing had happened, as though this enclave within the city, this prison of the Jews does not exist. He leads his children home, avoid-

ing the umschlagplatz and the train station, from which the first shipments of Jews to the East have already started. He leads them home safely, and he tucks them into bed.

'Please, Papa,' Bina says, sleepily. 'Tell us a story.'

He holds her close. 'What sort of story?' he says.

'A silly story!' Bina says, and Avrom nods his head very seriously in agreement.

Shomer kisses the tops of their heads, one after the other, and then he sits back and closes his eyes, and there is darkness.

And so he makes up a story to tell them; and for them, he takes out all the bad parts.

HISTORICAL AFTERWORD

BACK IN 2014 I published a novel called *A Man Lies Dreaming*, in which an Adolf Hitler who never rose to power ekes out a miserable living as a private detective in a London rapidly falling to a peculiar British kind of fascism. This was before Brexit or Trump, it must be noted: though the currents that led to both were ones I felt keenly back in late 2011, when I returned to England after an absence of some years.

A Man Lies Dreaming was a book I tried hard to avoid writing. Upon its unlikely publication it was, on the whole, well-received; which is to say, at least some people read it.

I had thought myself done with Wolf. Yet in the years since he kept revisiting me, and to try and exorcise his ghost I was forced, from time to time, to put down on paper some of his early cases.

The events depicted here took place between 1937-1938 and a year before the events recounted in *A Man Lies Dreaming*.

As preposterous as many of them may seem, they are solidly based in historical fact.

Red Christmas

WILLIAM JOYCE (1906-1946) was a leading member of Oswald Mosley's British Union of Fascists, serving as its Director of Propaganda. In 1939, and fearing arrest, he fled to Germany, where he became a naturalised citizen. He broadcast Nazi propaganda on the radio, and was nicknamed Lord Haw-Haw by the British media. He was hanged, in Wandsworth Prison, after the war.

Reinhard Heydrich (1904-1942) was one of the prime architects of the Final Solution (he chaired the Wannsee Conference), director of the Reich's Security Office (the SD), supervisor of the *Einsatzgruppen*, or Nazi death squads, and at the time of his death was the acting Protector of Bohemia and Moravia. He was a musician, a former naval officer, and a known womaniser. He died of his injuries following an assassination attempt in Prague.

Heinrich Hoffmann (1885-1957), Hitler's official photographer, was an early member of the Nazi party and owner of a photography studio in Munich. It was there that Hitler met the 17 year old Eva Braun, who was working as Hoffmann's assistant. Hoffmann himself survived the war, and died at the age of 72.

There were several leading ladies of Nazi cinema, though none of their careers much survived after the war. Elske Sturm is a composite.

The Lunacy Commission

BETWEEN 1939 AND 1941 the Nazis murdered some 70,000 people in their involuntary euthanasia programme. Aktion T4, as it came to be known after the war, targeted the disabled and the mentally ill, including thousands of children. The technology developed—specifically the use of lethal gas—would later be utilised in the death camps on a mass scale.

While Nurse Beil (meaning 'Hatchet') is fictional, she is based on real women. Pauline Kneissler, for instance, was just such a nurse, working at a euthanasia hospital in Germany where she could 'process' some 70 victims a day. Erna Petri, a mother of two, once found six small Jewish children hiding by the side of the road. She brought them home, calmed and fed them, then led them to the edge of the wood and methodically shot them. For more on these women and others, the reader may wish to pursue historian Wendy Lower's *Hitler's Furies: German Women In The Nazi Killing Fields* (2013).

Pervitin was the brand name of a form of crystal meth developed by the Nazis and shipped in large quantities to aid soldiers in the war effort. Adolf Hitler was a regular user. For more on the Nazis' industrial use of drugs, the reader may wish to pursue *Blitzed: Drugs in Nazi Germany* (2016) by Normal Ohler.

Killing Kiss

IG FARBEN—PURVEYORS, INDEED, of fine aspirin, heroin (trademarked 1895), toothpaste and, yes, pesticides—were the largest chemical and pharmaceutical manufacturer in Nazi Germany. Amongst their many profitable enterprises was the extensive use of Jewish slave labour, and the wholesale provision of Zyklon B for Auschwitz-Birkenau's gas chambers.

Wilhelm Rudolf Mann (who really did marry his cousin, proving Wolf right) had indeed joined the Nazi Party early. He was a board member of IG Farben, in charge of the pesticides department, and was behind financing the grotesque experiments of Josef Mengele in Auschwitz. He was captured by the Allies and put on trial for war crimes alongside his colleagues at IG Farben, but was acquitted. He died peacefully of very old age in Bavaria, long after the war.

The curious reader may wish to pursue Diarmuid Jeffreys' *Hell's Cartel: IG Farben and the Making of Hitler's War Machine* (2008) for more on this subject.

The Ahnenerbe was formally established by Heinrich Himmler in 1935. Herman Wirth was its first president. The institute gathered the worst of the Nazis' pseudoscientists, eugenicists, believers in Atlantis, "glacial cosmology" and, of course, the superiority of the Aryan race. As ludicrous as their work may seem, it was real, and had real-world and deadly consequences. The Ahnenerbe served to justify and provide a scientific rationale for the Holocaust. Bruno Beger personally was in charge of selecting prisoners to be murdered by gas simply in order for the Ahnenerbe to have a skeleton collection. Edmund Kiss joined the Waffen SS towards the end of the war but never stood trial. Erika Trautmann's Middle East trip involved spying for Nazi intelligence.

For more on the Ahnenerbe, the reader may wish to seek out Heather Pringle's *The Master Plan: Himmler's Scholars and the Holocaust* (2006).

A Wonderful Time

THE YOUNG ADOLF Hitler spent several years in Vienna, where he lived for a time in a homeless shelter and then in a men's dormitory. He was well familiar—though disgusted with—the red light district, and would have likely been familiar with the Saturn-Film Company. Cinema was effectively invented in 1895; almost immediately it gave rise to the pornographic movie. Saturn-Film, established by Johann Schwarzer in the early 1900s, was the first film production company in Austria. Among their pictures one can find *Forbidden Bathing*, *At The Slave Market*, *Female Wrestlers* and *In The Harem*, all of which are listed in their 1907 catalogue. The films were regularly shown in *herrenabende*, or 'night shows for men', much as described here.

Harvard-educated Ernst "Putzi" Hanfstaengl was one of Hitler's confidants during his Munich days. Following the failed Beer Hall Putsch in 1923, Hitler fled to Uffing, a small village in Bavaria, to the Hanfstaengls' home. The story is that when the village constable was sent to arrest him, a pale and wounded Hitler opened the door and surrendered saying, 'You must do what you must for your country.' Hitler went on to spend time in Landsberg Prison, where he wrote *Mein Kampf.* The rest, sadly, is history.

The Spear of Destiny

HEINRICH HIMMLER (1900-1945) was head of the S.S. in Adolf Hitler's Germany and one of the prime architects of the Final Solution, in charge of building and operating the death camps. On realising the war was lost, he tried to negotiate in secret with the Allies behind Hitler's back. He committed suicide while in British custody. Himmler had a lifelong interest in the occult, incorporating runic symbols and occult rituals into use in the S.S.

The notoriously anti-Semitic American poet Ezra Pound was an admirer of Hitler and a devoted follower of Mussolini. He was arrested for treason after the war, spent 12 years confined to a psychiatric hospital, but died of old age in Venice in 1972. Margherita Sarfatti was Mussolini's long-time mistress and his propaganda adviser. She left Italy in 1938 and for a time was a costume designer in Hollywood. Harry Cohn was the last of the great moguls of old Hollywood, and was said to have a signed photo of Il Duce on his desk—at least until the beginning of the war.

The author Harry Stephen Keeler was indeed very fond of the appearance of skulls in his intricate and highly implausible novels. It is said he visited London at least once, though under what circumstances is unknown. I like to think it would have gone something like the way it is recounted here.

Adolf Hitler really did view the Holy Lance at the Hofburg in Vienna in his youth. Years later, the Nazis did acquire the same artefact, but their main motivation seems to have been simple financial gain. The spear was returned to Austria by General Patton following the end of the war.

* * *

THERE COULD BE no Wolf without Shomer, of course. As I mention in my notes to *A Man Lies Dreaming*, Shund, or Yiddish pulp fiction, flourished for many years prior to the war, and an author by the name of Shomer was indeed one of its prolific practitioners. That Shomer, however, died peacefully in New York City in 1905; long before the Holocaust.

I am indebted to Jason Sizemore of *Apex Magazine* for publishing both "Red Christmas" and "The Spear of Destiny" (originally published under the title of "My Struggle"); and to Maxim Jakubowski for publishing "A Wonderful Time" and "Killing Kiss" in *The Book of Extraordinary Amateur Sleuth and Private Eye Stories* and *The Book of Extraordinary Impossible Crimes and Puzzling Deaths* respectively. "The Lunacy Commission" is original to this collection.

ABOUT THE AUTHOR

LAVIE TIDHAR IS author of *Osama*, *The Violent Century*, *A Man Lies Dreaming*, *Central Station*, and *Unholy Land*, as well as the Bookman Histories trilogy. His latest novels are *By Force Alone*, children's book *The Candy Mafia* and comics mini-series *Adler*. His awards include the World Fantasy Award, the British Fantasy Award, the John W. Campbell Award, the Neukom Prize and the Jerwood Fiction Uncovered Prize.

FOR NEWS ABOUT JABBERWOCKY BOOKS AND AUTHORS

Sign up for our newsletter*: http://eepurl.com/b84tDz
visit our website: awfulagent.com/ebooks
or follow us on twitter: @awfulagent

THANKS FOR READING!

*We will never sell or give away your email address, nor use
it for nefarious purposes. Newsletter sent out quarterly.